The Princess Seeks Her Fortune

Mary Catelli

Published by Wizard's Wood Press, 2018.

THE PRINCESS SEEKS HER FORTUNE

First edition. May 24, 2018.

Written by Mary Catelli.

Chapter 1

The voice's querulous tone rose from the courtyard, and through the window with the still chilly spring air. Then some words came through clearly.

"You could stand being more like Alissandra!"

Alissandra sighed and looked at the half-finished shirt in her lap. She could finish it in a quarter hour if she put her mind to it. She folded the cloth up and put it away before turning to the women about the room, bent on their sewing.

"I have to bring the clothes to the orphanage."

The women looked back, most unmoved, some contemptuous at her flight. The maid Lizina—a woman her own age with moon-blond hair and gray eyes that verged on white—rose and curtseyed in silence. Alissandra nodded gravely. The castle had taken on Lizina years ago. At times, Alissandra had to remind herself how dangerous it was to ask where someone came from; she might be a lady and take offense. And Lizina helped her with the orphans' clothes. She should just appreciate her.

Alissandra headed toward the door. She had a chance, just a chance.

. . .

"Really, Aunt Donata," said Queen Olivia, her voice cool and regal, "Esmeralda already has three princes wooing her. Without our locking up her sisters in the kitchen for fear of her losing them to them."

Alissandra winced. In the stairwell, the air still held the winter cold from the castle stones. She walked down. They would not leave, and she had to face them in the courtyard, to get by. She could get through it, she told herself, without being cornered.

Out in the courtyard, the sun had warmed the air, and four figures stood in a familiar scene. Dark-haired Queen Olivia looking almost stately, Princess Esmeralda with fiery hair and her face set in annoyed line, Princess Iolande with pale brown hair and mousy manner, Donata hunchbacked, with enormous eyes and swollen thumb, such that no one dared to be rude to her.

Esmeralda tossed her hair and gave Alissandra a contemptuous glance. After a moment, so did Iolande. Olivia gave her a cool smile. Aunt Donata's smile seemed more pleased, as if she did not realize that Esmeralda and Iolande would be the worse for the chiding—

And why not? thought Alissandra. It wasn't Aunt Donata that they sniped at.

"Ah," said Esmeralda, her lip curling, "the perfect little Princess Alissandra, with her perfect golden hair, her perfect gray eyes, off to show off the perfection of her character—like a little angle—by bringing clothes to the little orphans. How—old-fashioned."

"You are free to join me, if you like," said Alissandra, woodenly.

Esmeralda snorted and tossed her head again, like a blooded stallion. "And be so out of date? You're as bad as Aunt Donata—and you're not a third her age."

She turned to Donata, her lip curling again. "At least I didn't spend every coin given to me for my dresses on some peasant lass's funeral."

Alissandra forced her breath in and out. They would never, ever, ever forgive her that.

"My dear daughter," said Olivia, "the orphans are perfectly well clad even without your offerings. Your needle would be better put to work in the castle. You can sew things fit for a dowry chest."

A shameless attempt to make her stay and argue. Her mother knew as well as she did that her dowry chest was filled to the top—and that if Iolande and Esmeralda cared about theirs, they knew the cure. Alissandra walked past.

At least they did not follow.

Esmeralda called after her, "You can't be the *perfect* princess. You're the *middle* one."

Iolande laughed. Then the wall cut them off. Lizina joined her in gathering together the clothes into two bundles.

"I should set out to seek my fortune," said Alissandra, her voice low, as she folded up a small shirt.

Lizina cocked an eyebrow.

She folded more for the pile. "Yes, it will be trouble—I'll end up scrubbing pots in some kitchen somewhere—if I don't end up hired by cats—and they don't make me do the housework here—but seeking my fortune could end up better, after being worse."

"You might end up hired to watch over a corpse instead," said Lizina, dryly, as they wrapped up their piles for the bundles.

"True enough," said Alissandra, "but I'm not the youngest, or as brave as a bee. It would frighten me to death when the corpse moved." She hefted the bundle. None too heavy—she was not letting the pile grow too large between deliveries. She could probably carry Lizina's as well, if a princess could go alone anywhere except to seek her fortune.

Which, she thought, she *would* do if they made her fill up her sisters' dowry chests. She let out her breath and went back out.

Queen Olivia stood alone in the courtyard and tried to look queenly. "Alissandra, you should stop this posturing. We all know how you ended up without a gown, the first time we sent you for one."

Alissandra tried not to flinch; she thought she managed to hide it. "I still have to bring the clothes." Her mother's mouth pursed, but she did not argue.

Looking swiftly about picked out the garden with snowdrops and pale apple tree blossoms, and her sisters in it. Esmeralda, rubbing her knee, was glaring at a bench.

"Stupid bench," she said.

Alissandra turned away. No sign of Esmeralda's wooers. For their own sake, she should be glad they had wisdom enough to avoid the garden.

She went on. Through the back door, down half a dozen steps, press against the wall to open the secret door and fumble in the niche for the lantern. She lit it as Lizina stood in the doorway, awaiting the light.

The yellow glow sprang up, gilding them, their bundles, and the stones about.

"This is one thing that no one has told me," said Lizina, coolly. "Why the lantern? It's not underground, it has windows—it is bright enough to find our way."

"Bright enough to see any traps?" said Alissandra. "You do know what happened to King Leonardo?"

Lizina closed the door, cutting off the daylight behind them. The lamp seemed brighter. "He used the tunnel to reach his secret bride, because he could not bring her to court."

"And?" said Alissandra. "After that?" She started down the flagstones.

Lizina's voice was very dry as she followed. "You have not only a secret husband, but jealous brothers-in-law? Who envy him so fine a bride? Who would lay a trap for you here to tear you up with knives? Or broken glass?"

Alissandra lifted the lamp; the stones here were uneven. "I have sisters. They would call it a jest even if they broke my neck. One could wish they had so pleasant and human a motive as jealousy. Esmeralda has wasted more money on horses—" She let her breath out. Esmeralda ruined the horses and abused them as stupid wastes of money. Yet that waste never kept their parents from letting her buy more horses.

"Besides," she added, primly, "I don't have a husband to discover the magical cure for my injuries despite my blaming him for them." She looked ahead.

The lamplight showed the stairs, and Alissandra descended with care. The stone beyond had to be the same pearly gray as the rest of the castle, but it looked darker and darker. At least, she reminded herself, the spell King Leonardo used to speed his passage was gone. They could walk at an ordinary pace. The little windows, up at the roof level, might indeed have let in sunlight enough to walk by, but she was still glad for the lamp.

She trudged on. Her thoughts roved back.

"You'd think," she said, "that I had given away the kingdom. Bad enough that a fair and pleasant land has a law that would let *anyone* refuse burial to a corpse until the debts are paid—let alone those *ingrates*—to insult me because I paid those debts—"

She bit down her words and closed her eyes for a moment. She remembered it like yesterday. The chapel among the apple trees, the new-turned earth of fresh graves beside it, the pale petals flying like doves on the breeze, the candles lit about a coffin in the chapel. The guard who begrudged her every word, but admitted that the dead woman had helped them all with her goods when illness struck before succumbing herself, but still they would not let her be buried until all her debts, contracted during her illness, were paid for.

Alissandra forced her breath out and opened her eyes. The castle had hired Lizina after that day, but she had to have heard it all. Many times, no doubt—Alissandra had heard the smirking maidservants telling new maids the tale with conspiratorial whispers. Lizina might not be so sick of hearing it as she was, but that did not say much.

After a minute, Lizina said, "Would you do it again?"

Alissandra turned to glare at her. The lantern, shining slantwise, cast more shadows than light across Lizina's calm face.

"What else could I do?" said Alissandra.

Lizina looked calmly back at her.

A minute later, the stairs appeared ahead of them, and Alissandra hurried. Best to be about her business—it would be a better distraction. And who knew? By the time she returned, Esmeralda might have taken a horse and gone tearing about the countryside. Or perhaps a wooer would occupy her.

With the lantern in its niche on the other side, they walked out into daylight and the square where houses of fishermen faced them. Children paused in their play—at least the younger ones—and a chicken flapped, squawking, from their path. The play of water sounded.

They came about a corner, to where the water splashed down into the pool, and a ragged beggar girl, her dark shawl slipping on her shoulders, fumbled for the dipper. Already, her skirts were dark from splashes of water spilling down. Alissandra frowned. After a moment, she realized the girl had to be blind.

"Can we help you?" she said softly.

The girl turned her face toward her. "I am afraid of falling in the water," she confessed.

"That is no problem, then," said Alissandra. She glanced at Lizina, who smiled and took the bundle from her. Then—the little tin dipper hung from its nail, and it was a moment's work to fill it.

"Hold out your hands so I can give you the dipper," she added. "The spring water is very cold, and I do not want to spill it on you."

The girl took it, and drank, before handing it back, and saying, "How gracious you are. May you comb roses from your hair and wash lilies from your hands whenever you wish to do so, with sweetness enough to overpower ever foul scent."

Alissandra opened her mouth and shut it again.

"May you marry a good king, and may you live in good deeds always." The beggar girl smiled with uncanny calm. Alissandra swallowed. The girl's bare feet showed no signs of dust.

Alissandra turned to hang up the dipper, and felt unsurprised to see no sign of the girl when she turned back.

A wide-eyed little girl, and an even smaller boy, from the orphanage, gawked at her, however. The tale, thought Alissandra gloomily, would be about the city in minutes.

"Come along, children," said Lizina. "These clothes will not walk into the orphanage on their own."

That at least made them move, but it did not stop the wide-eyed stares, or coax any words from them.

Once inside, the orphans scampered off. The sisters took the clothes with solemn gratitude. Sister Apollonia gravely showed them the garden where the orphans frolicked, to see how they prospered.

In one garden, the girl was crying as others swarmed about her. "I did see it, I *did*!" She looked about, spotted Alissandra, and hurtled across the grass. "I did see it! There was a *lady* at the well and she looked like a blind beggar girl and when you helped her she gave you roses and lilies. I'm not a liar!"

Sister Apollonia drew in her breath sharply. Alissandra's heart sank. She *did* tell the truth.

"Then," said Alissandra, flatly, "go fetch me a comb. Or a basin to wash my hands in."

The little girl's eyes brightened, and she scurried off. The little boy toddled after.

Sister Apollonia said, "Your Highness, you should not encourage them—"

"To tell the truth? It's a good habit." She looked contemptuously on the children where the girl had stood. They shrank back. "With *those* ones discouraging it, it is very seemly to encourage it."

The little boy hurtled over the grass, with a comb in his hand. Alissandra caught him before he tumbled on his face, and took the comb. The girl inched her way across, trying not to spill the bowlful, and so Alissandra leaned to one side and shook out her hair. The orphans, knowing nothing of how old-fashioned such princessly hair was, oohed over it.

The little girl reached her. For all her care, her hands and sleeves and skirts were wet from splashing. Alissandra, her mouth twisting, had her put the bowl on the grass, and then combed.

For a moment, as the strands slipped through the teeth, she thought herself a fool. The beggar girl might have been just a beggar, posing as a lady to make herself feared.

Then her comb reached the end of the strands, and roses fell. Single roses of deep red about their yellow hearts, double white ones, many-petaled roses streaked with red and white like a carnival—and she had only to breathe in to smell the sweetness.

The orphans, and the sisters, were still.

She had shown that.

She sat on the grass, laid down the comb, and washed her hands. Lilies fell free. Lilies as white as swan's wings, as yellow as sunshine, and both as sweet as the roses.

She let her hands drip droplets and lily buds. Half a dozen lilies were enough to show the truth. Then she carefully gathered up the flowers before the gawking orphans and handed them to the little girl and boy.

It took a moment for the girl to beam.

* * *

In the shadows of the tunnel, Alissandra took up the lamp again. "I think," she said, "that we shall mention nothing of the well back at the castle. Not even to the servants."

Lizina raised an eyebrow. "It is likely that the rumors have already reached the castle."

"The news is not going to reach Esmeralda or Iolande because of what I say. Or you say."

Lizina nodded. Alissandra let her breath out. She had heard of times where the lady—or the lord—had found two girls who managed to pass their hidden tests, and one not, but more often when anyone who tried to ape the first girl failed.

She never heard of a tale where all three succeeded.

She dared to hope as they walked back. Her sewing was so much less interesting than Esmeralda's horses. If Esmeralda had ridden off, she might be somewhere she could not hear the tale. Iolande would never dream of trying to ape her without Esmeralda's encouragement.

And trying to win the favor of a lady like that was so old-fashioned. Esmeralda would be more likely to jeer that Alissandra had tried it.

At the end, she slipped the lamp away into its niche and opened the door. Her sisters stood like sentinels there.

"What," said Esmeralda, her arms crossed, "is this story about your combing flowers from your hair, and washing them from your hands?"

* * *

Queen Olivia hovered by the door. "I can send a maid with you. . . ."

"Iolande and I will suffice," Esmeralda said as she donned her mantle. "It is neither that dark nor that cold, and we know better than to descend on the well in force. We're not *fools*."

"Guards or maids might offend her," said Iolande.

"We won't do that just to please Alissandra." Her lip curled as she glanced back at where Alissandra sat. "No matter how much she thinks being first makes her special."

Alissandra folded her hands in her lap and wished she could slip out. It was not as if either of them would be affected by any argument she could offer.

"We'll do *better* than Alissandra," said Iolande. "Roses and lilies and violets and tulips and asters and—not just one or two flowers."

Alissandra sat like stone. Esmeralda swept out the door. Iolande scurried after.

Queen Olivia sighed. "You must stop sulking, Alissandra. If your sisters are bold enough, you are not entitled to stop them. It ill-becomes you to be jealous of your gifts."

Alissandra kept her hands neatly folded in her lap.

"You are being ridiculous. Not every princess has her story told after her—only those whose lives are interesting. Let your sisters get their gifts, and it will be too dull to repeat. Your father and I do not get talked of, not when I did not have to flee my father, or have the maidservant supplant me on the way, yet we are as happy as my father and mother were, for all that she came from an enchanted orange and then spent time trapped as a canary. And if you had listened when your governess taught you history, instead of caring only about the tales, you would know many more."

Alissandra stood. She had learned her lessons, but that, or any other retort, would only prolong this scene. As if the danger to her sisters were the lady and not her sisters themselves. Fortunate Lizina, dismissed to work as soon as her mother had arrived to find Esmeralda interrogating her.

Queen Olivia scowled. "I should send you to study it. A prince will want a bride well enough versed in history to help him govern his kingdom."

"I," said Alissandra, "will tell a maiden to bring the annals to the sewing room on the morrow. I will even go now to see what volume."

Her skirt swirled about her, and she swept back along the gallery, looking neither right to the portraits nor left to the garden. She barely heard the doves cooing, there or as she climbed the stairs into the library.

With the window overgrown with ivy, their spring leaves touched the light with green, though it was not so dim as full summer. She looked warily about, but she was indeed alone. And there she stood, breathing hard.

She should read the annals indeed. Her father would not give her a gown like all the flowers in the fields, another like all the birds in the air, and a third like all the stars in the sky. Nor was there any talking calf eager to help her. Roses and lilies would not provide for her if she ran away to seek her fortune.

She looked at the annals. Perhaps she could read tales of princesses who escaped without taking such things with them. Her mouth twisted. Certainly princesses lived who had managed without them, but those sensible ones had not left until forced.

She was leafing through a seventh volume and idly thinking that she should put the first one back when a maid scurried in and curtseyed.

"Yes?" said Alissandra.

"It's Prince Hans, Your Highness," said the maid, wringing her hands.

The first of Esmeralda's wooers to arrive, the one from farthest off, the very model of courtesy—the maids had giggled over his fair hair and good looks, but Esmeralda had scorned him as the very picture of an old-fashioned prince.

"Yes?" When the maid said nothing more, Alissandra added, "What is wrong?"

"Why, Your Highness, he's *packing*, to go!"

For an unsettling moment, Alissandra felt as if she had stepped on a stair that proved not to exist. Packing? Leaving? Before Esmeralda—

That thought calmed her. Prince Hans showed more sense than she had guessed.

"Are the servants helping him?"

The maid gaped.

"Speed the parting guest—it is only courteous. I should bid him farewell."

The maid sputtered. "King Frederick, Queen Olivia, we couldn't find either."

"What? Would they hold him captive? I dare say that it would be courteous of them to bid him farewell, but perhaps he has news from his father and must leave at once, being needed in the kingdom." She shrugged. "And packing will take some time. Farewells are still possible."

When the maid did not move, she added, "Go, aid the prince. At once."

The maid curtseyed and scurried off.

Alissandra sighed and sat back. So Prince Hans left. Esmeralda might even be just enough to rejoice at repelling him. Her gaze moved about the room, picking out this book and that one. Esmeralda had not, after all, sent the princes off on impossible quests, even when they bragged of slaying wizards and ogres in her service, or ordered them to do impossible tasks, or asked impossible riddles, and cut their heads off if they failed.

Esmeralda might, on the other hand, sulk that he had not waited to be rejected. It seemed more likely.

Alissandra stood to put her books back. The last volume slipped into its place when the door opened with a bang. She jumped.

From the doorway, Esmeralda glared at her with hatred, as if Alissandra had tried to murder her.

"You!" Rotten vegetables and rubbish fell from her mouth. "This is all your fault!"

"Your fault!" said Iolande.

Chapter 2

"Enticing me like that!"

King Frederick winced at the reek. With all the windows open, the breezes could still not clear the chamber of foul air. And, garbage falling from her lips, Esmeralda raved on.

Without, Alissandra noticed, saying what had gone wrong and gotten her cursed. Her stomach roiled at the stench, and she turned her face away. Both of them had managed to be courteous to Donata—

"Like that," said Iolande. Nothing fell from her mouth, but not once since their return had she done anything but echo Esmeralda.

A maid stole by in the corridor. Alissandra grabbed her arm—her nose wrinkled—and told her to fetch a comb.

"Look!" said Esmeralda. "She's trying to sneak off!"

"Off," said Iolande.

"She knows she should be punished—you should never have let her off so lightly for squandering her gown money on that foolish funeral." Esmeralda turned a fearful scowl on her.

"Patience, my child," said King Frederick. "A king must not judge swiftly. It causes his subjects to hold him in contempt."

Esmeralda choked. In the silence, a blessed breeze blew from the window. Alissandra walked over to it.

Outside, with grave faces, John and Ivan approached by the garden path. Then the wind shifted. Their faces contorted in ghastly expressions, and they scurried off.

Hans was wiser, thought Alissandra.

Then Lizina came down the corridor. Foolish, when she might face Esmeralda's rage for having been with Alissandra—but Lizina held the comb in her hand.

The first roses, a gentle red and a delicate pink, fell. They looked incongruous among the muddy-colored garbage, but the scent was suddenly of sweetness. Alissandra looked up.

"Dear," said Queen Olivia, "it's not nice to show off."

"I'll stop," said Alissandra, "if Esmeralda stops increasing the problem."

"You shall not," said King Frederick, straightening. "You shall dispel the reek whenever it arises. It is unreasonable to expect your sister to keep silent when you can accompany her and cure the problem. As if she had to save her seven brothers from a curse by keeping silent seven years! You shall not curse her so."

Esmeralda smirked.

Alissandra's eyes narrowed. Close enough, she decided. Dancing attendance on Esmeralda would be as hard as sewing to fill her dowry chest for her. Worse. Sewing was worthy in itself.

"Until the day we find a way to break the curse."

"Don't be absurd, Father," said Esmeralda. Foulness spread again. "Only a simpering old-fashioned princess would wait for a rescue. Iolande and I will rescue *ourselves*."

"*Ourselves*," said Iolande.

Esmeralda turned to sweep out, without quite watching where she went as she picked her way through the rubbish. She collided with the door. "Stupid door," she muttered, mud dripping, and headed out, with Iolande following.

Alissandra combed her hair, but a dozen roses later, she curtseyed. "The maids will need to clean this before it hardens. I will send them." She left before they thought to forbid her.

Outside, a lingering Lizina curtseyed. Alissandra repeated her message.

"The housekeeper is already summoning the maids, Your Highness," said Lizina, with a little smile.

Alissandra nodded and walked along the corridor.

Lizina accompanied her. "There's talk among the servants. It seems that our princesses went to the wall at the north of the orphanage."

"They don't even have a door there," said Alissandra. "How could either have thought that was *before* the orphanage?"

Lizina spread her hands. "There they went. There is a fountain there, with a lame old woman by it—"

"Everyone knows that when some lady plays that trick, she changes her seeming! Not every time, but often enough. How could—" She shook her head. And her mother thought *she* had not listened to her lessons!

"The Princess Esmeralda was—very angry at the time."

And so more foolish than usual. Alissandra sighed. "Bear the news of the roses. Then come and aid me in my packing. All the maids will be helping the princes, no doubt."

* * *

Esmeralda did not let the grass grow under her feet. If Alissandra had not happened to glance out the window at the right moment, she would not have realized that her sisters were already stealing off with their packs. (Without even Esmeralda muttering and raising a stench.)

Her own wardrobe and chest lay open for reflection. She had not even started to take things out. Then, she told herself, her problems were less urgent.

"Your Highness." Lizina curtseyed from the doorway.

Alissandra straightened. "Lizina. You came as a maidservant from a far village. I need to know what would be prudent to pack, setting out for a long journey across the kingdoms, to find a place." She eyed her clothes. "Especially since I have no coins to buy what I need."

"Drab," said Lizina, firmly. "It will not show the dirt at work or on the way."

Alissandra bobbed her head and obediently sorted out the drabbest clothes—most already intended for travel. "I wish I could demand things in return for my marrying some odious suitor, before I reneged."

Lizina lifted an eyebrow. "A dress like all the flowers in the field, a dress like all the birds of the air, a dress like all the stars in the sky? To travel in?"

"Those first, of course, but I was thinking of the chest that flew over land and sea. Useful for travel." She stretched her arms over her head. "Though I would have to pick and choose what to pack, still." She sighed, lowering her arms. "And the uproar will make it difficult."

* * *

Maidservants whispered about the princesses and horrors among themselves. As Alissandra walked closer, they fell silent, as if they did not realize how the stone echoed.

Then, the rumors about riders would be more accurate. She walked past the maids, toward the great chamber. Her father would be too busy to notice her, especially—she took a side door into a narrow, window-less corridor—if she took the route he used to get ready for audiences, and came in from the back.

She did, just as half a dozen riders, dusty from the road, came in through the front, great door. They bowed before King Frederick and Queen Olivia. Prince Hans, Prince Ivan, and Prince John, she noted, stood to one side.

Her mouth twisted. Prince Hans, too, had difficulty leaving in the uproar.

She stood to the others side as if she had been summoned. A rider with his blue cap in his hands recounted how they had followed the princesses and found their tracks in the wild and even spied the princesses themselves, walking through a meadow filled with wildflow-ers.

Which was how they saw them engulfed in a black mist and whirled away, leaving no tracks.

"The path where they walked, it was muddy. We could have seen anything they left. They had left tracks up to the last moment."

Alissandra, slowly, let her breath in and out. Whisked away. Had she left on the same day, what would have happened to her?

Her parents and the princes alike were silent. After a minute, her father dismissed the riders with a hollow-voiced gratitude and solid coins.

As soon as the door closed, Prince Hans drew a deep breath and bowed. "Your Majesties." His voice was like ice. "I do not see how anything you, or they, have said changes anything I have set out to do." His face set, he looked at them for a moment before he went on, "Surely, your fair daughter can rescue herself." He bowed again and went out the door. His footsteps echoed down the corridor in the silence. Then, outside, the wind blew, and the canvas banners cracked in it, hiding the sound.

Prince John said, softly, "As if Princess Esmeralda would marry a man who rescued her. I would think her more likely to strike him across the face."

And Prince Ivan, who had talked the loudest of dragons and ogres and savage bears, looked pale and said, "Do you even know that she needs rescue? She could have cast the magic herself."

Her, thought Alissandra and felt unsurprised that none of them remembered Iolande.

Chapter 3

Alissandra slung on her pack and drew a deep breath. The morning was gray even without mist, as gray as the stone of the castle, but she had daylight enough walk without breaking her neck on some root, she could travel all day, and she was even leaving before Prince Hans—if she hurried.

Servants would be moving about the castle, though. For once, the front stairs offered more stealth than the back ones.

Out the door, down the corridor—past the empty rooms where her sisters had once slept, to the stairs—she crept closer to the door, and down below, the clock ticked out the moments, the noise growing.

At the bottom of the stairs, Lizina stood with a pack at her feet.

Alissandra, her hand on the railing, stood still. "Are you a princess who ran away from her father because he tried to marry you?"

Lizina's lips curved into a cool smile. "No. But the other maidservants are whispering that I said I could rescue the princesses."

Alissandra winced. She did not know that her father would believe them if—when—he heard, but she could not think Lizina a fool to escape before. "And not that you could spin a roomful of flax in a night?"

"I can't do that, either," said Lizina, but she smiled. She picked up her pack. Alissandra hurried down the stairs as she slung it on.

A voice rang down after her. "What are you up?"

Alissandra flinched and looked up at her father, still in disarray from waking.

Her mother, close behind him, said, "I never believed it, when the maid told us—"

"Why," said Alissandra, "*what* could be more old-fashioned than setting out to seek your fortune?"

"When you are the only heir to the throne?" said King Frederick.

"What throne?" said Alissandra. "You've offered half the kingdom to whoever it is that rescues Esmeralda and Iolande, and the whole after you die. That hardly leaves so much as an inch for me."

"You knew you would not inherit before, but you did not leave then."

"Then," said Alissandra, "my staying would not cast doubt on the sincerity of your reward. I could not risk my sisters thus."

"The reward is sincere."

"What? Shall I never marry, then? What is the point of my remaining if I have no heir of my own? We'd end up like that kingdom—" She waved her hand southward. "Orre. My governesses held up Orre as a warning. Where the princess had a nose a foot long and never married. She got to be queen, but then they had to hunt down a cousin to succeed her. You can hunt down the cousin now."

"Of course we will marry you off," said Queen Olivia.

"To the first beggar who comes along, to humble my pride?" said Alissandra. "Won't do. Even such a marriage will lead princes and peasants alike to conclude that you do not mean to give the kingdom to their rescuer." She continued down the stair.

"You can not leave against my will," said King Frederick, thunderously.

"Esmeralda did. And Iolande." Alissandra took up the door latch.

As soon as the door closed behind them, she pulled up her hood to hide her face. Lizina did the same beside her. They hurried along the way for a minute before they heard her father bellow behind them. Alissandra flinched, told herself not to be a fool, he would never have been shocked for long, and walked faster. She opened the side door, and they reached the street. She let out her breath and hurried along it. Noting the signs on the way—the Blue Bear made her roll her eyes.

"I should have had them make me a bearskin cloak," she said. "One that would—somehow—turn me into a bear. I could have hidden in it, as a disguise. And I would not have had to hide in the woods; with you coming, you could pass me off as a marvelous beast and show me off at fairs."

Lizina's mouth twitched. "Oh, that would not do at all," she said solemnly. "You would tell me that I had to sell only you, and never your bridle, you would tell me again and again, but one day, someone would persuade me—offering me ten times as much gold for it as for you—"

"True enough," said Alissandra, as they passed by . "It does always turn out that way. Perhaps it's just as well."

"Where were you planning on going?"

"North and east," said Alissandra. She turned by a bakery. "That's the closest border. And one of the thinnest. Once past that, I can look for a place and hope I find one before I am reduced to eating thistles raw."

"It is not a little thing, to go behind the borders," said Lizina, as solemn as a governess.

"Enchantments, ogres, lords and ladies, talking foxes—" She stopped for a child running, bucket in hand, to the well. "My governess would enumerate all the reason why anyone would be a fool to ever leave the kingdom. But nothing ventured, nothing gained." She drew a deep breath. "Merchants favor this road. You can even cross it in a day if nothing happens."

She stopped and looked at Lizina, who said nothing. "And my sisters show you're not even safe without leaving."

Lizina nodded. They hurried on down the streets and past all the stores and houses. Gray morning lightened toward eggshell yellow, and more and more people stirred: servants about their errands, tradesmen opening their shops, vendors hawking their wares to both. Alissandra thought that this crowd could hardly mark two drab women scurrying along, but when the final bridge came into view, with escape in sight—the river ambling beneath, between rushes and newly leaved willows, the fields beyond greening with spring—she glanced nervously at Lizina.

Whose face was as serene as a candle flame in a room without a breath of draft, but. . . .

"You don't have to come."

Lizina raised an eyebrow.

"Across the border—I know it can be dangerous—but they aren't looking for you. They're looking for me. It's not the refuge for you that it is for me—"

"Their Majesties," said Lizina gravely, "saw me with you. And I know which way you go. No, I think my safety calls for me to go."

They started to climb the bridge's stone. I ought to argue with her, thought Alissandra.

"And I've saved my wages," said Lizina. "I have coin. Let us share our good and evil fortune as we go."

Alissandra did not know how to argue with that. She glanced down at the river, where fishes darted through the murky water, and then the bridge began to descend.

On the other side, the road lead up into hills. Upward all the way, Alissandra remembered.

She glanced about to ensure no other travelers were near. "I brought some jewelry," she said, her voice very low. "I have broaches like the sun, the moon, and the stars. Not easy to sell, but may be useful at need."

* * *

The day turned clear and bright, and for the season, warm. In a forest glade, the trees had only a haze of green where the leaves were new, and daffodils and crocuses bloomed as bright spots of yellow and violet among the dead leaves.

Just a glade, thought Alissandra, not yet the true forest that marked the border. Her heart still pattered more quickly than before.

Coming out of the trees did indeed reveal a village. It stood surrounded by fields, but beyond the fields lay the forest, close enough that it was not just a dark line on the horizon. The trees were clear, and they would reach it soon enough. A merchant cavalcade watered their mules and horses—and selves—at the well as the last of their number came forth from the forest. They must have traveled it in the day already.

"I wonder how far it is to the castle, on the other side," said Alissandra, forcing the words from her dry mouth. "Royal service is, after all, an old tradition."

"The kingdom is not that large," said Lizina. "It can not be that far off. Once we get through the forest."

"As ever," said Alissandra. "Miss Smithson was passionate about all the horrors we could expect." Her mouth twitched. "Making us learn how borders are liminal, and all the ways that liminal lands draw enchantments. Why, it was so dangerous that she would never ever ever cross the border to visit her own sister, who married abroad."

"Never?" said Lizina. "One wonders if perhaps something else would help her decide that."

Alissandra shrugged. "Likely enough, but Miss Smithson truly did not like the magic."

They skirted the cavalcade, where even the merchants, let alone the men, were dusty from the road. For a moment, she wondered what they had seen, but things changed quickly in the forest. News might lead them astray.

They reached the forest, unnoticed by merchant or villager, and slipped within, onto a dingy gray-brown dirt road. Trees closed in to either side, with boughs spreading over their heads, and the bright green of new leaves casting a slip of shadow on them. Great flocks of birds twittered among the trees, and leapt up in swirling cloud as they flew onward.

The sun inched onward, more slowly than Alissandra would have believed possible, but walking was warm enough. She threw back her hood before long, and, not much later, pushed her mantle back from her shoulders.

Lizina walked along in perfect calm. Alissandra let her breath out and remembered a time when an ancestor of hers had returned—with a bride. And then. . .

"I wonder. . . ."

She more breathed it out than spoke, but Lizina glanced at her.

"This might be the road that my great-great-great-grandmother walked on—three times—" She scowled. Her governess would be ashamed. "No, one more great. Queen Olivia."

"There is a Queen Olivia in the portrait gallery," said Lizina, mildly. "One who was not your mother, even without being an older portrait, dressed in older gowns."

That Lizina had looked through the gallery intently enough to know the names somehow did not surprise her.

"My parents are third cousins," said Alissandra. "My mother is named for her. But my great—her husband the king found her in the forest without her hands—"

Lizina's eyebrows shot up.

"The portrait was much later. He married her without her hands. And then—" She waved her own hands in the air. "What had happened was, she was a princess. Her own brother wanted to marry her, and when she demanded to know why, he raved about the beauty of her hands. So she cut them off and sent them to him in a silver bowl. He had thrown her out in the woods. That was where King Heinrich found her. But when he married her, the queen mother, Queen was not happy. A strange woman of unknown birth, perhaps a peasant."

Lizina raised an eyebrow.

"Some people do care," said Alissandra. "Want the prince, or king, to marry a princess. There was a queen once who wanted her husband to promise that if he remarried, it would to be a great princess—but—" She shook her head. "That was not King Heinrich, he had not married before. Still, his mother cared.

"So when he had to go to war against Queen Olivia's brother, and Queen Olivia gave birth to a beautiful baby boy, the queen mother sent word to the king that she had given birth to a puppy."

The road wound upwards, past an ancient oak, crusted with grayish lichen, and its trunk thicker than some cottages she had seen. Beyond, the trees were set far apart, their boughs forming a canopy that showed summer would leave all in gloom. Even now, with the new leaves, there was as much shadow as sun.

"The king sent back word that she and the puppy were to be well cared for. Perhaps he thought that Queen Olivia had wished for any child, even a puppy, and it would work out in the end.

"But the queen mother was not to be thus thwarted. She forged a letter ordering Queen Olivia and the little prince to be abandoned in the woods. The queen mother's servants did not dare disobey for fear that the queen mother would do worse, and so she was lost in the forest again."

Alissandra drew a deep breath. Perhaps not so early in the year, and certainly not near a road.

"She drank at a spring soon after, and her baby slipped into the spring. When she fished about trying to get him, she pulled him out again, and found she had hands to do it with. Then a white deer came to her and helped her, so she lived in the forest until the king came back.

"His servants asked about the cruel orders before he reached the castle and his mother's tale about their sudden deaths, and the carefully prepared false grave. He threw her into a tower prison and searched for Olivia, and found her again, and brought her back."

"On this road?"

Alissandra shrugged. "Could be. More likely just my fancy. Since it is a road between kingdoms." The towering trees still spread on as far as she could see.

A bird, trilling, darted across the way. Alissandra trudged on with Lizina until she picked out, in the distance, a post of some kind.

"What's that?"

Lizina's eyebrows went up, but she ventured no guess.

The way diverged into three paths before them. A sign post, aged and weathered, had arrows pointing toward each one—none back—and while she *thought* the sign post had had paint on it at one time, no one could have read any of the arrows. Not even someone who knew what they said already, and had only to pick out the words.

"I thought," said Lizina, "that a milestone with the words carved in was traditional."

"That would be for things like 'Whoever goes this way will lose his life, but his horse will live' on one, and 'Whoever goes this way will live, but his horse will die,'" said Alissandra. "Much too long to fit on these signs. And we don't have horses." She sighed and eyed the trees. "So it's no more useful—and no less—than if we had no sign post at all. We have to choose a way."

Wind rustled leaves and tugged on her hair. Lizina looked at her and offered no opinion.

"A stone would be more useful," grumbled Alissandra.

"It would always be true," said Lizina. "Whatever way you go, you will die in due course, but unless you drop dead the moment you step on the path, you will live, too."

Alissandra's eyebrows went up. True enough. She looked down each way. Trees and vague hilly shapes—none looking like a sleeping giant—or having smoke rise from a dragon's lair.

"The middle one," she said. "As good a rule as any. The median between two extremes." She hitched up her pack and walked onward. Lizina walked along, and the crossroads slowly vanished behind them.

"I wonder if we will see any wolves, anyway," said Alissandra, idly.

"You haven't got a horse to feed one," said Lizina.

"We'd need two, anyway."

A bird twittered among the trees.

Alissandra pondered. "Or perhaps not. If a wolf could carry both Prince Ivan and Helena the Beautiful—" A painter had done their portrait so, both seated on the wolf's back, as the annals had said they had when they escaped. It had been their granddaughter who married King Giovanni and became *her* ancestor—and brought the painting for the gallery. She shrugged. "—surely one could carry two maidens."

"No doubt we'd be glad of it before the day was out," said Lizina.

Alissandra shifted her pack. She would be glad of it now. Especially since the way rose ahead of them, steeply enough to remind her of why merchants preferred mules to cart. And to remind herself stand straight.

The trees still surrounded them, but among them appeared rocks, and even small cliff-faces—no higher than her waist, sprouting ferns and moss that hid the weathered stone. Climbing higher meant that the cliffs grew taller, rising to the left hand and descending on the right, until trees often grew below their feet, laying out a veil of green as fine as a most delicate princess could wish for.

In the clefts of the rock, doves cooed. Alissandra paused for breath and looked for the nesting birds. She saw motion, and a glittering bit of silver catching the light as if the doves, like magpies, had treasures in their nests. Then a dove shifted again, and her breath came out as she saw: the birds themselves were silver. Every feather caught the sun as the doves cooed, and billed, and nested, and sent light glinting here and there.

Alissandra finally collected herself and looked at Lizina. The other woman, with a faint smile, studied the birds as well. Alissandra drew in a steading breath. Time to go on, she thought, giving the birds one last glance.

That was when she saw the snake.

It slithered up the cleft, long and thick as her arm, its eyes dark and glittering, its scales muddy brown shades. It did not even hesitate when she spied it, with its gaze intent on the birds above it.

Her breath coming low and fast, Alissandra looked about. A stone, rounded, fit easily into her hand, and hurtled easily through the air to crash against the snake.

A whole truelove of doves surged into the air, their coos like the tolling of bells, their flapping wings filling the air with sound as they wheeled about and about, sunlight glinting from silver wings.

Until a feather, glinting, fell through the air. It tumbled through the air, twisting and turning. Its flight seemed to hesitate in midair, just as it reached her height.

She put out her hand and caught it.

It gleamed in her hand, reflecting sunlight and her own face, looking upon, and the cliff beyond, with the ripples through the quills. It felt odd, as if it could be made like an ordinary feather and made of silver as well.

The doves settled again on the cliff, and she drew a deep breath. Lizina smiled, faintly.

"Silver," said Alissandra, "but not, I think, for sale."

"Wise," said Lizina.

Alissandra put it away in a pouch. And it was not midmorning yet.

"The sort of thing," she said softly, "that you would sell only for the way to the bridegroom when the troll-wife is holding him captive. . . ."

* * *

Noon saw them down from the hills. The track went on, along a stream. It had bounded, foaming white, over rocks and cliffs as they descended, but here it ambled and meandered under the trees, or among brush that sometimes hid the forest behind, as their leaves had grown more quickly than on the trees. The shadows kept the forest almost chilly at times.

But they could always walk on the track.

Alissandra and Lizina came around a bush set with milk white flowers. A pond spread before them, out to willows with their early leaves still yellow green, thick on their hanging branches. Past it was another pond, and between them, a narrow neck, barely wide enough for the path.

They plodded along the bank. Quiet surrounded them as they came about the willows.

The pond on the other side—was not a pond but a lake, Alissandra realized. Its far bank was indistinct with distance. The waters reflected sky and cloud, and on the shadow sides of faint waves, showed glimpses of dark water. Bird after bird swam on it. Wedges of elegant swans swimming serenely; gaggles of geese bobbing on the wavelets, and sometimes with their tails in the air as they fed below the waves.

No maidens bathing, noted Alissandra, no white clothes that would turn them back to swans if only they were not stolen.

Around another promontory, a duck paddled on the lake, in and out of shadows, and glinting golden where the sun struck it. Behind it streamed the ducklings. Three—six—a dozen—Alissandra counted two dozen before the dazzle of the gold left her silent and wondering.

"Still on the border," she murmured.

Lizina smiled. Alissandra wondered how many borders Lizina had passed before she found her post at the castle, and what wonders she had seen on the way.

But for now, the duck and ducklings swam and almost glowed.

Across the waves, a dark snake, brown as mud, slipped through the waves, its dark eyes intent on the last ducklings.

Her breath drew in sharply, and she looked about. No loose stones, not even ones too small to distract or too large to lift. But there, a downed branch—

It hurled through the air and splashed against the waves. The duck rose up in the air, quacking, and all about the lake, swans and gees rose, their wings hammering at the air, and the geese honking to add to the ruckus. The duck settled behind the ducklings and chivvied them on-ward.

Alissandra could see no sign of the snake. Not since the branch hit. She let her breath out.

The duck took wing again, arched about the shore, near the branches, and flew over the bank where they stood. A single golden feather fell, doing loops in the air until it hovered before Alissandra. She grabbed it.

"I grow richer and richer in things I can not sell," she said.

"Have you ever heard of a princess selling such things and prosper-ing after?" said Lizina.

"Ah, but I have not heard of selling such thing at all."

* * *

Noon had passed before they reached the lake's other side. The path wound upward, though not so steeply as before. The trees to either hand slowly turned to firs, growing thickly together. They left the path darker than the path behind them would be at midsummer. The scent of the dead needles, carpeting the forest floor in amber, filled the cold air. The brighter forest retreated behind them until there was nothing but gloom and shadow before and behind.

"If nightfall finds us here," whispered Alissandra, "how would we know?"

"Let us hope to wonder forever," said Lizina, gravely, but not much more loudly.

Alissandra nodded, and walked more briskly against that fate.

Then she stopped. Light flared along the path, but only a spot of it, and fiery red and orange—it was no sunbeam piercing the boughs.

"A fire?" Alissandra said.

"Odd to have a fire at this hour. Even for—"

She did not say it, but Alissandra's stomach roiled. "Even for ban-dits," she said.

"Or," said Lizina, "something else that we have not guessed." She let her breath out. "Perhaps we can sneak by."

Alissandra nodded. They walked on as softly as they could. The fiery glow increased, and then a song, wordless and rich, rolled toward them. Alissandra stopped. The glow increased. Alissandra ran, her heart hammering, as she scarcely dared to hope.

The firebird swooped among the branches: scarlet, yellow, orange, every feather agleam with fiery shades, and its song curled on and on. Alissandra, gawking, had to take a step backward from its brilliance and beauty. It circled about trees, flitting in and out and turning shadow to light.

"So this is—"

That was when Alissandra saw the snake coiled about a branch, its muddy brown scales not glinting even in the firebird's light, its dark eyes fixed on the bird. She looked frantically about for any stick or stone, but only gnarled roots and dead needles spread about the forest floor.

No stone—and in a hurry, she reached for her belt pouch. Her mouth tightened as she hoped it was enough, but she hurled her moonstone brooch at the snake. The gemstone glittered in the fiery light and smashed against the snake.

It hissed and shifted, and the firebird flared. Alissandra's arms flew up to guard her eyes, her head turned away, her eyes closed—and the light still left her blinking, and her eyes watering.

She barely saw the fiery feather, gold and red, descending through the air before her, though it hung on the air.

Chapter 4

Out of the firs, the forest again turned bright with spring, the small leaves barely shadowing the way. There was no warning from shifting light as they walked about a stand of maples, and found pastures, broad and green, where lambs frolicked, and spring wildflowers were merry in violet and yellow and pale blue.

"Not even sunset yet," said Lizina, pleased.

"Which does explain," said Alissandra, "why the inn is not yet in sight." She hitched up her pack.

Lizina shrugged. "We want to get as close to the city as we can. Though by this path, it won't be a single day's journey."

"What?" said Alissandra. "When I have a firebird's feather in my belt pouch?" She waved a hand in the air. "I don't even have a talking horse to warn me that if I give it to the king, he will say that if I could do that, I could get him the whole bird."

Lizina smiled. "Or to tell you how to get the firebird after you ignored its advice. Still, it would be easiest in the city, to find a place."

Alissandra's nose wrinkled, and she trudged onward. Scullery maid or the like. It would be a place. Or perhaps they could sew and sell their wares.

After many minutes, she said, "I think this is King Matteo's kingdom."

Lizina nodded.

She tried to summon up other memories, she must have learned more from her governesses, but even walking half the day had left her too weary to care as long as they reached a village before sundown.

* * *

Birches, their bark as white as swans, lined a broad stream. The path wound up the banks as the sky turned rosy and orange, until it led them to a village. Off in the distance, Alissandra thought, there stood a castle tinged with sunset shades, but the distance was far too far to travel in what was left of the day.

The village would be a town if it grew much more. A mill on the river, its wheel churning along; a sprawl of houses with children playing, chickens clucking, and women spinning on their thresholds; a smithy billowing smoke; and among them, one great building with a sign hanging in front of it: a golden crown, and the inscription, The Princess's Rest. Her eyebrows went up. How often did princesses, even ones out seeking their fortune, rest here? It had to have enough room for a cavalcade of them.

Though, she reminded herself, the number of travelers, not the size of the village, determined the size of an inn.

She glanced about, trying to pick out the main road. After a minute, she picked out at least seven of them, heavily traveled by the wear, and broad enough for any merchant's caravan. Unsettled, she looked back to the inn as they approached it. If so many travelers came, she wondered if the inn were large enough for when they came in force.

"Welcome to the Princess's Rest!" A rosy-cheeked man, built like a bear, came out. He waved his hand at the sign. "The famous inn, built in the days of Princess Rosine, and she was our good King Basil's great-great grandmother, and since he was King Matteo's grandfather—how time passes—I trust you have heard that it was only in her day that a traveler could stay the night by telling the tale of his journey. Nowadays, it is run by myself, the humble Master Bernardo, and you must pay in coin."

Alissandra blinked and tried to remember. That was the way that a princess had learned how dead giants had come to lie about her castle while all within had lain in an enchanted sleep, but not here, not this close. This one must be—

"Not even all her days," she said gravely. "Only until one brought her news of her husband." It exhausted her knowledge of the place, but Bernardo looked pleased.

"I dare say," said Lizina mildly, "that even in her day, some preferred to pay coin than to reveal such things."

"But we would rather be paid as we are looking for places," said Alissandra.

His eyebrows went up, and he looked her over.

"I can cook and bake and build fires and sew and mend," she said. "And I've always learned quickly whenever set to a new task."

Lizina laughed. "I can build fires and change beds and wash linen and scrub and sweep and sew and mend—and she is right, we ran away to seek our fortunes and may as well ask at once."

His mouth pursed. For a moment, Alissandra wondered whether he took them for sisters—Lizina's looks were at least as close to hers as Esmeralda's or Iolande's—and then, whether he would hire them both. She might be glad enough to scrub pots by the time she found a place, and she hoped she would not have to go on without Lizina. She shifted her weight and hoped he took them for devoted sisters.

"I'll see what you're made of, now," said Bernardo. "The baker could use a hand, what with the baking being so delayed, and the maids with the beds—"

"Where should we lay our mantles and packs?" said Alissandra. "The baker will have my head if I bring dirt into the bakery."

* * *

Her hands still wet and cold from washing under the pump, Alissandra stood in the bakery. An apron spread over her travel-stained clothes. Lizina had left as soon as her hands were clean, but Alissandra had no time to miss her, between stirring and kneading and rolling and shaping, and eventually putting the loaves into the fierceness of the oven and coming away sweating.

She had barely had time to notice that the baker's name was Kate, and only as she pulled away from the oven she did ponder, even briefly, what foreign princess brought that name to this country.

Kate did not set her to more work while the bread baked. Alissandra leaned against the white-washed wall, and waited. Once or twice she eyed the fire, but it had been well built, and the logs burned hot enough without more. The bustle was not enough to turn her from her thoughts. The bakery would be far hotter in the summer, with standing back then being little more relief, and she had only a time or two made that much bread at the castle, but she suspected this was a light load here.

But she needed a place, and—she had yet to win it. The bread still had to come out, though the oven had not asked her to do it before the bread was burnt. One could not count on a talking oven.

Minutes later, with the wooden peel, she pulled out the loaves one by one. Good plain brown bread, such as they made back at the castle to be sure of having enough for the beggars.

She wondered if they made white bread as well. She could bake that as well, without even having been turned into a frog first.

Kate merely set her to make the next batch of brown bread. As hours passed—the church bells chiming them out—she wondered how many more batches the kitchen would make before Kate pronounced the work done. Her arms ached, and her feet, and Lizina's advice about the dress had already gone awry, with the way drab showed up flour.

Then, abruptly, Kate sent her out with two buckets to the pump. Finding the stable boys already pumping water, Alissandra gratefully let down the buckets to wait. The sky was still lit, red and flaming orange, the blue overhead darkening but not dark. Birds still flitted about and warbled, and a bundle of tumbled white linens came across the courtyard. It took her a minute to pick out Lizina behind it, and she did not think that Lizina saw her.

Then she had not had time to think so much as that if this kingdom had had a King Basil, it was likely that the king was descended from Vasilisa the Wise as well as she was.

The stable boys went to take their water.

She supposed it could have been Vasilisa the Beautiful, instead. Alissandra went forward to pump her buckets full, and try to avoid being splashed by the icy water.

Bernardo stood with Kate when she returned, her skirt as much wet as dry.

"She'll do," said Kate.

Alissandra forced her breath in and out, caught between elation and the knowledge that she would drudge like this for days or weeks or years. Or a lifetime. A princess who stayed in the scullery never made it into a tale.

Remember your place, she told herself, and bowed her head, murmuring her gratitude.

Kate nodded. "Give me a month with her, and I won't be shamed, leaving you to marry John Miller. Bad though it was to put off the baking this late, we got through the batches swiftly enough—it'll last us a week."

Alissandra's breath gushed out. To bake like this only once a week—that she could certainly endure.

Bernardo nodded. "You'll want to clean up before the dinner."

Alissandra hesitated. "Lizina?"

Bernardo laughed. "She did well enough, too. As the newest, you twain will share the attic room. Until the inn is too full, and we all end up sleeping in the straw."

Alissandra smiled, and found herself remembering that in the morning she would truly have to rise with the rooster, and get right to work.

Chapter 5

In the morning, they had actual light to dress by—dim, gray light—but Alissandra did not doubt that winter, or cloud, could take that away for future mornings. Today, they could manage. Even as stiff as she was—

"I need a paler gown," said Alissandra, pulling her skirt straight. "One that won't show flour as plainly."

"Very true," said Lizina, dryly, pulling on her own, charcoal gray gown. "I wish I had one to lend you."

Alissandra shrugged and went to put up her hair. "It's part of your laundry duties. When we get our wages, no doubt I'll know which seamstress I can go to. Unless I have time to sew it up myself."

Lizina nodded. Then, Queen Olivia had always given her and the other servants lengths of cloth for Christmas and Easter. They had to sew them up, she had never noticed how long it took them, but it was cheaper than buying the gowns.

As eating the servants' breakfast here would be cheaper. She put in a final hairpin, more than she had ever used before, and hoped the pins, and hair, would stay up.

They slipped down the stairs, and Alissandra was glad of the dance masters who had taught her to be light on her feet.

A voice drifted up. "They said she did the laundry whiter than clouds. Or snow. Or swans' wings—"

They reached the door. Other servants, gathered round the porridge pot with their bowls, fell silent. Alissandra's gaze went down toward the floor, but she went to get her own bowl.

"Slept well?" said a groom.

"Rested like a princess," said Alissandra.

They roared with laughter.

"That was the rest the princess gave, not that she got," said Kate. Alissandra realized she must look blank, but she did not know what to say, and Lizina looked, as always, as serene as candle flame in still air. Kate's eyebrows went up, and she dished herself some porridge.

"What?" said a small girl, her face as sharp as a rat's. "You hired on without knowing the story?"

"As long as the story isn't that Bernardo doesn't pay his servants, why would I wonder about it?" said Alissandra as the servants filed by the pot.

"But this inn was founded by a princess!" said the girl, standing by the pot and waving her spoon.

"That might even make it dangerous to ask," said Alissandra, gravely. "Did some—lady help her? Or some lord?"

The girl scowled.

"Get your porridge, Finella," said Kate.

Finella shrugged and spooned it up. "Well, it was. She married a crab—a golden crab—but the king didn't like it, so he made him build a castle in a single night, and gardens and birds, but when he did it, she had to marry him—and he turned into a man at night so she was happy—and the king and queen didn't like having their daughter married to a crab, so the king had a tourney to get her a good bridegroom, and the crab came and won—he was a man then—and she let slip that the knight was the crab." She waved her spoon in the air.

"I can see her point," said Kate dryly. "With her own mother fussing and fuming about how much more she wanted Princess Rosine married to that gallant knight in golden armor. But—" She turned to Alissandra. "The mother found his crab shell and burned it, and he vanished."

Alissandra drew her breath in and forced it out again. She wondered if the mother had an ancestor who was freed by the burning of his animal skin. She had heard of those tales, too.

"So," said Finella brightly. "She built an inn. She told everyone they could stay the night if they told her stories of their travels."

"For news of her husband, she hoped," said Kate, sitting down. "It worked. In time, in time."

"If," said one groom, "you could count as 'working' having to go div-
ing down into a pool, hiding out in a castle, and tricking your husband
into coming back after you broke your word to him—"

"It'll do," said Kate.

Alissandra sat with the rest and ate. Without a scrap of honey. It
wasn't burnt, she told herself, and tried to eat as quickly as the others.
And not wonder if her father could have found her sister by now if he
had built an inn.

She scrapped the bowl when it occurred to her: neither of her parents were young enough for that sort of quest. And neither of her sisters
had a wooer who would go after them. She stood with the rest to put
the bowl aside.

"Lizina, Alissandra," said Kate, peremptorily. "Come with me. You
will help with porridge for the guests."

Alissandra's arms remembered the hours of mixing and the heat of
the ovens. Still she nodded. Kate led them to the corridor to the main
room, and voices muttered behind them about sisters or stepsisters.
Alissandra wondered how Finella had been quelled from asking them
if they were.

Kate murmured, "There's another tale, too. That's the one the travelers will ask about."

In the common room, the great pot was coming to a boil over the
fire. Kate hurried to it, without a glance aside, though across the room,
on the wall, was a feather as long as Alissandra's arm, broader than her
outstretched fingers, and more iridescent than a peacock's, with red and
orange as well as blue and green and purple glinting through it.

Kate looked up from the pot. "That's what they ask about."

Four travelers, dressed for the road, eyed them all as they came in,
and Kate nodded toward the window. Stacks of bowls there—Alissandra and Lizina went to bring them over.

As Kate ladled out the porridge, she went on. "That's the ogre's
feather. Once upon a time, the king ailed and needed the ogre's feathers

for a medicine. A brave young man said he'd do it, and set out. He came to this inn, where the innkeeper and his wife had but one child, a daughter, and she had vanished."

Alissandra handed out the bowls, but travelers followed the first four, and she and Lizina had to scurry, to unpleasant looks and mutters of how it took them long enough. And more footsteps sounded on the stairs.

Lizina took the next tray. Alissandra told herself that she would grow accustomed to the work. Even if many travelers had no interest in the tale. She took up the tray.

After the first rush, Kate said, "So he went on from this inn and came to a village where they had a marvelous bird, all red and green and gold, but it had lost all its color and stopped singing."

Three travelers pushed back their bowls and rose. Alissandra scrambled to fetch the bowls to the scullery.

"So," said Kate, "he told them he would find out what he could. After them, he came to a river where the ferryman asked him why he had to ferry and ferry and ferry, without rest. So he promised this as well, and went on to the mountain where the ogre lived. There he found the ogre's home, but only a young woman at it, stirring the pot."

A clatter on the stairway had her stirring her own pot, and Lizina and Alissandra scrambling to serve bowls and clean away those where the traveler was done, until the next lull. The porridge pot was more empty than full, Alissandra noted with relief. Then she reminded herself that they might need another batch.

"So," said Kate, "the young woman asked what he was doing, and whether he knew where he was, and whether he realized there was no escape. The only reason the ogre kept her was to cook his stew. The young man told her that he had come for two of the ogre's feathers, and though it cost him his life, he would not leave without them. And whatever he could do for her, he would do.

"She told him she would do what she could for him, though he could never aid her. She hid him away in the pantry, and the ogre came growling back, declaring he smelled human flesh.

"The woman told him it had to be a bone that a crow had dropped down the chimney and nothing more—she had had to clean it up—and stew would be late because of all her hard work. He should lay down his head in her lap and rest while it cooked."

More travelers arrived, and the bowls went out. The room got quite crowded, all the more in that some were not rising from their empty bowls.

Perhaps they awaited friends, thought Alissandra, returning from the scullery to find no more empty ones waiting.

"The ogre snored away," said Kate. "Without a moment's pause. The woman pulled out one of his feathers. Woke him right up, and he was all growling and snarling, and she said that she had been dreaming, and must have pulled it out in her sleep. She had dreamed of a ferryman who could not leave off ferrying. The ogre grumbled that he had only to leap off the ferry before his passenger, and the passenger would have to ferry instead. What a fool, almost as much as *you*."

Kate dished up a few more bowls, and eyed the pot. Alissandra thought of a larger batch and managed to not groan.

"So the ogre went back to sleep, and the woman pulled out another. This time she said she had dreamed of the bird. The ogre said a snake was poisoning the air about it, and if they dug up its hole under the bird's cage and killed it, the bird would soon be bright and sing again.

"The ogre went back to sleep, and the woman put a log under his head instead of her leg, and gave the young man the feathers and told him that the answer to the innkeeper was that she was his daughter, and the ogre had carried her off in a mist, so she did not know how to leave. The young man told her that he had not come in a mist, and could get her away, and safely, too.

"They reached the ferryman, and told him they would tell him once they were on the other side. They did, too, and he offered to take them elsewhere, but they hurried on. The ogre woke up and chased after, but the ferryman offered to carry him over, and as soon as they reached the other shore, he leapt out, and so the ogre had to ferry forever.

"They told the town how to revive the bird, and the innkeeper that she was his daughter, and so the young man went on alone to bring the king the feathers. His doctors made the medicine with one, and it worked, so the young man took the other feather back with him, and all the silver and gold the king gave him, and married the inn-keeper's daughter.

"Bernardo is their great-great-great-great-grandson."

At that, half the room, it seemed, got up. Had they all listened? wondered Alissandra, but first she had to run all about gathering empty bowls.

"One wonders," said Lizina, "why they didn't rename the inn. The feather is more striking than the tale of the princess; easier for a traveler to recognize, and he might even doubt the other."

Kate laughed. "When we are done, go out the front door and see the castle the crab raised. All pink and orange like the dawn—and the chroniclers will assure them that it's all true."

* * *

Not until mid-morning could they escape the inn's walls, and Alissandra felt keenly aware that the venture into the cool air would only last for moments. The sky was filled with wispy clouds and others in rows like fish scales, half promising rain for the future, but not that day. Still, she looked over the fields. The castle did indeed stand in shades of peaches and roses, like the dawn.

She turned back to the inn. Belinda, the butcher's daughter, having delivered the meat, was standing very close to Bernardo and, with a little smile, was whispering to him. Bernardo looked over the courtyard.

"Ah, Alissandra! All set to tell all the travelers the tales of the feathers, and why the inn is called the rest?"

Alissandra nodded. "For those two, yes. Are there no other tales of the inn?"

"Not here, not here," boomed Bernardo. "Too wise, too wise—you know how all the tales of innkeepers talk of how they are fools who steal enchanted treasures until they get what is coming to them." He shook his head. "A table that covers itself with food, an ever-filled sack of gold—it's all fun and profit until you get a stick that beats you without mercy, or a chair you can't rise out of." He did not so much as glance aside, and Belinda pouted and moved off. "There's no such tale about the Princess's Rest."

"There could be tales of someone who stayed the night here," said Alissandra, lightly.

"Who would care to mention it? The closest we came to such a tale was a time when a young man complained that his companion had taken all his luggage and gone off, but he chased after him, and I heard nothing more of it." He shook his head. "I was only a boy, and I remember it best because the young man was handsome, but his companion was an ugly soul, all hollow cheeked and pocked face, except for his marvelous glossy black hair."

"Aye," said an old groom. He shook his head. "Such a marvelous marvel, that hair and that face together."

Alissandra let out her breath. "It was a wig."

Bernardo looked at her.

"The young man—his name was Jean, and his parents were poor. No one in the village would be his godfather. They asked another poor traveler to do it. Turned out that this man was a foreign king in disguise." And my great-grandfather, she thought.

"So!" said Bernardo. "He came through here to find his godfather."

"Even so. Alas for him, the king sent him a letter, and it warned him about three foes of the king: a bald man, a cross-eyed man, and a mangy man. If any such man tried to travel with him, he should do without their company. He escaped the first two, making excuses and getting away, but the third wore a fine wig, and tricked him, and stole all his luggage. Only when he reached him, Jean knocked his wig askew, but the mangy man got a sword to his throat, and made him swear to serve him and never tell man or woman what he had done. So the mangy man used Jean's letter to pass himself himself off as the king's godson."

A dove in the apple tree by the door began to coo, a deep tolling sound. Alissandra thought of the kitchen, and all the baking.

"Well?" said Bernardo. "If the tale ended there, you would hardly know it well enough to tell it."

"How wise you are." For a moment, she thought of looking around to see who else listened, but the thought of finding herself goggled at from all sides dissuaded her. "The king, King Nicholas, had a daughter named Helena, who had been carried off by an ogre. And the mangy man told the king that his servant was so wise and competent that there was no doubt he could retrieve the princess. Jean tried to object, but the king would not listen.

"He went down to the sea to lament his fate—even if he found a way to win her away, the mangy man would find another way to kill him."

A stable boy stopped next to Bernardo, who shushed him.

"A dwarven man came to him there, and asked him what he was about. Jean told him, and the dwarven man told him to ask the king for a ship with three decks, one full of crumbs, one of dead beasts, and one of honey—and to take him on as his crew.

"The king eagerly did as Jean asked, and the mangy man could hardly complain—he tried to jest that Jean could do it without them, but Jean said it would be unwise to try. And so they sailed. And sailed. Until they came to an island where no one was visible, and yet a voice asked what they had to sell. The dwarven man said, Honey, and the voice said, What joy. A thousand ants, and a thousand more, and a thousand more, swarmed the ship. They left not a drop of honey, but they told Jean that he had only to call on ants to gain their aid.

"Then they came to an island of ducks, which bore off the crumbs, and one of ravens, which bore off the carcasses, and with an empty ship and those three promises, Jean sailed on to the island of the ogre, where he found the Princess Helena chained in a cave, with a chain of gold, a chain of silver, and a chain of copper. She told him that he had to challenge the ogre to win the keys, and the ogre would set him impossible tasks, so he had to flee and save his life, since he could not save her. The ogre ate any ship that came near.

"Jean said that he had only one death to die."

Half a dozen servants openly watched her, and even some of the guests. She faltered, and went on. If Bernardo did not hurry them on to their work, it was not her place.

"He greeted the ogre at the mouth of the cave, told him how he had come there, and said that he had come for the keys. The ogre told him he could have the copper key if he could find it, and if he could not, within a night and day, he would forfeit his head. So the ogre threw the key into the shore, where the sands swallowed it up, and went into the cave.

"Then Jean summoned the ants, and the ants carried away all the sands until he found the key.

"The ogre said it was all very well, he had had pity on him because of his youth and folly before, the next one would be less lenient. He threw the silver key into the ocean. Jean summoned the ducks, who dove down into the waters until they found the key and brought it back.

"When the ogre saw that, he accused Jean of being sly and crafty, feigning idiocy to win his pity, but now he was wiser. So he threw the gold key up into the air, and it did not come down. Jean summoned the ravens. They told him it had caught on a cloud, rose up in a great flock, and brought it back, but giving it to him, warned him not to tell the ogre that he had it. Jean took the three keys and unlocked the chains, and he and the princess fled to the ship, and the dwarven sailor set sail and bore them back to her father's castle. Everyone rejoiced. The king spoke of marrying her to his godson, who had brought so useful a servant.

"Princess Helena said it would not do, that people would not respect him as a prince or as a king because of his face, but she had something from her godfather that would amend that. She built up a fire and put a pot on it, filled it with water and added some herbs, and when it boiled, she declared that her bridegroom must leap into that. The one who did so would be so handsome that his subjects would respect him.

"The mangy man looked at the pot and ordered Jean to leap in, to test it. Jean did so, and leapt out again, uninjured, and so handsome as to amaze them all. The mangy man leapt in, and was scalded so badly that he could not leap out, and died in pain.

A skitter of laughter went about the courtyard.

"His wig fell off, so that King Nicholas said, that is no man, that is the mangy lord who would be my daughter's godfather when she was born.

"Princess Helena told how she had heard Jean tell the ogre his story, and he was made welcome as the king's godson. They told him how four lords had sought to be Princess Helena's godfather—a cross-eyed one, a lame one, a mangy one, and a dwarven one—and at the advice of the wise old aunt who was her godmother, he had chosen the dwarf.

"And the dwarf himself came, because he had been the sailor, and to join the wedding celebration of Jean and Princess Helena. They reigned after King Nicholas and had three daughters and a son, who is now King Frederick now."

And, she thought, has three daughters.

Bernardo roared with laughter. "That's how young I was. Right over the border and I never put together how the tale ended."

Servants and travelers laughed. One of them murmured that the mangy lord had been a fool, not to listen and notice that Princess Helena had said *the one* who jumped in would get it. Alissandra smiled a little. She had seen the keys when small, when her grandmother had sat her on her lap to tell the tale, and her grandfather had brought them out to show her.

Martin, the stable master, bellowed about laziness and slackers, and sent all the grooms and stable boys running about, readying horses, but few others moved onward.

One traveler said, "There's a tale from there now, about how all three princesses vanished—"

"Only two," said Alissandra. "One princess met a lady and was courteous, and got flowers and well-wishes. The other two tried the same, and got cursed for rudeness. They set out to rescue themselves, and vanished."

Silence fell. A chicken clucked in the dusty road, and a servant carrying a bucket said, "You'd need a fine realm to make me take one of *them* in marriage."

"What about the third?" said a maidservant.

"Oh, she left to seek her fortune, since her father's kingdom goes to the rescuer of her sisters." She said it lightly, but all sorts of speculative gazes turned on her.

Lizina appeared, her arms full of sheets, and as if a thread had broken on puppets, their gazes turned away. Grooms led out horses, and travelers turned to take theirs, or demand to know why theirs were not ready yet.

Alissandra let her breath out. It was well that she had fled with Lizina; going together helped hide where she had come from.

And the bakery had, no doubt, things to be baked.

"I heard the princes who were wooing the older princess left without so much as trying to find them!"

"One had to leave—Ivan—his father died."

Baking, thought Alissandra. If rumor happened to tell the truth at the moment, she could not count on its doing so about anything else, and rumor would not bake a single loaf. She nodded to Bernardo and headed toward the door.

"Princesses got to be careful about that," caroled one travelers. "Or they end up like Princess Long-Nose." He jerked his thumb, toward another road.

Alissandra calculated her geography as best she could. Yes, that way would lead toward Orre, where Queen Aurelia had died, ancient, unwed, and childless—she had barely been old enough to remember, but she had learned it in her lessons—but the queen's notorious arrogance might have had as much to do with that as the nose.

Even if the cursed nose had not sprung from the arrogance. Her governess had insisted it had, but then, she had been trying to curb unruly princesses at the time.

* * *

Ah, changes.

Today she worked with delicate dough, to make fine pastries. If enough wealthy travelers came by, she supposed it was worth the effort to bake.

At least, there was less of the dough. Even if she had to be more dainty in her handling, and do as little as possible to shape it.

Kate, with folded arms, leaned against the wall and watched. Which was the actual point of it. At times being the baker of the Princess's Rest meant needing to know how to make such pastries.

No sooner had Alissandra carefully poked the pastries to sit by the oven, not too close, to rise, than Kate straightened.

"I'll keep an eye on them. You'll need to fetch water for the fillings."

Alissandra nodded wearily. Lugging water would be the hardest work of the bakery. Except, she thought as she picked up the bucket, she would probably be glad of it at the height of summer, to escape the heat.

Warmth was already rising as she waited. Though, come summer, she would rise early, in the dark, to bake before cock's crow. A ruby butterfly fluttered over the courtyard, and two stable boys whispered that she had managed to impress Kate.

"It's just baking," said Alissandra sharply. "You just have to know how to do it."

"But Kate—Kate—" One boy waved his hand in the air, as if trying to show a vague shape. "Her parents came with Queen Lilyrose—Princess Lilyrose she was—to marry King Piedro, when he was a prince."

"Her brother and sister *still* bake at the castle," said the other.

"Well, then," said Alissandra, "I can see where she learned to bake." She turned to the pump, and soon had water sloshing into her bucket. Odd it was, to be one of those hearing the tales, not the one that tales were told of.

It happened, she told herself, and picked up the bucket. Some even said it was two generations between tales.

Chapter 6

The morning was cloudy and gray, but Kate did not seem to mind. Neither did her bridegroom, Giovanni Miller.

In spite of herself, Alissandra glanced at the bridal cake. No one had eaten any yet, and in looks at least, she had certainly succeeded. She still found it strange that, even after her confession that she had never baked one before, Kate had entrusted it to her.

Shrieking boys and girls ran over the grass, only to be rounded up by an anxious mother who did not think mud would add to to the festivities.

Three boys darted off, into the mill. The mother looked harassed. "Could you—"

"Of course," said Alissandra.

Inside, in the shadow, she had to blink and wait for her eyes. Though the mill was not grinding, the air was still laden with dust. Alissandra's mouth twisted. Even today, her violet gown might show the flour; she had thought she would have one day of escape where the sober color, which would not show dirt, was an advantage. And she might have to twist up her hair. All very well to wear it down, maidenly, at the celebrations—

Bright hair flashed in the corner. "Ho," she called, and crossed the planks of the floor to where the small boys tried to hide.

"Ho, indeed," said a deep voice from deeper in the mills. "What is this?" The old Pietro Miller came slowly out a doorway.

"Hunting!" said Alissandra. "For small boys who escaped the festivities outside."

He chortled. "They should have warned you where you roved." His hand swept out, to the narrow stairs. Her eyebrows went up, but she walked over. Before she was halfway up, the great fireplace was clear, and so were the boys wrestling with the stones, unable to budge them, though their fingers tried to pry into every nock.

"As if," said Pietro Miller, "that would not be the first place anyone would look."

Slowly, with dark looks at the miller, the boys drew back.

"I concede my father was not the wisest or most prudent of men, but anyone know the tale knows that could not be said of my mother."

"She gave him them," said the oldest boy, sulkily. "He had adventures."

Alissandra glanced between them.

"Huh," said the boy. "*She* doesn't know. With all her tales about godsons and ships—telling her tale over and over—like there aren't any tales about anybody but royalty."

"I could tell you about a farmer's son who won a wizard's daughter's hand in a game of cards," said Alissandra. "And how he chased all over to win her, because the wizard tried to renege. But that's not the tale folks ask me for."

"But. . . but. . . but—" said the youngest. A shaft of sunlight fell over his face. "He's got a wishing hat! And a purse of gold—it's always full! And a horn that summons soldiers."

"Now you are being silly," said Alissandra. "Everyone knows what happens when you steal things like that. It's like a curse. The thieves end up quarreling over who gets them, and some wayfarer manages to trick them out of them in the guise of settling the quarrel. They're lucky if he doesn't kill them all."

"We wouldn't," muttered the middle boy, with no conviction, and they let Pietro and Alissandra usher them out the door and ran off toward the festivities.

"I'll tell you one day," said Pietro. "It came out in fits and starts, so there are a lot of partial tales about." He smiled a little. "It even has a princess in it."

"I'll tell you the card game tale, if you wish," said Alissandra. "Later, after we ensure they do not tell tales of how you missed signing the marriage papers."

* * *

On the grass, beneath the trees, the tables were festooned with garlands and laden with food. At the head table, Kate was rosy and bright, and Giovanni watched her with joy.

And just a trifle of impatience. Alissandra drank more cider. There would, of course, be a ruckus, to let the bridegroom and bride slip off, but she would be hard put to recognize the signs at a commoners' wedding.

Down the table, a boy regaled them all with how she did not know what was in the mill.

"Heavens," she said, sharply, "you ask so much for the tale of the mangy man and the ship that you give me no time to tell any other, let alone ask for yours."

Pietro laughed. "A time for tales is hard enough when you are hard at work, baking."

"Tell it now, Uncle Pietro!" said a little girl. "I want to hear it again!"

A chorus of childish voices rose in agreement.

"Then," said Pietro, "I might—if Alissandra Baker tells the tale of the card game."

It drew every gaze to her.

"Yes, I know more tales," she said demurely. "But age before youth—let Pietro Miller tell his first."

His mouth twisted, and he glanced sideways at her.

"Yes, yes, yes," called the children.

"Once upon a time," said Pietro, magisterially, "a young man, not so wise, set out to seek his fortune, with not a thing more than his name of Giovanni. And he came to a mill that was not running. The miller had died and left his daughter Guillametta all alone. So he helped her, and got the mill running again, and when he went on, she, in gratitude, gave him three things she had found in a chest: a purse, a horn, and a belt.

"And he walked on and on, and was hungry, and when he saw an inn, he said, 'O if this purse were filled with gold!'"

"And it was!" shouted a little girl, wriggling.

"So it was, so it was," said Pietro. "He went on and on, staying at inns and paying in gold. He came to the kingdom where they had a lone princes, and her name was Aurelia, and she was beautiful, so beautiful, as beautiful as the day is long, and she had never accepted a wooer. So our Giovanni fell in love—and what can a man not achieve, with all the gold he could wish for? Even if the king did not need a loan!"

Everyone laughed. Yes, that was the easy way to win a princess with gold, thought Alissandra. This young man had the advantage that he didn't have to win the purse by not bathing for seven years.

"So he bought a fine house and wore fine clothes and gave fine dinners, and one day the princess from her balcony called for him to come to her. At the door of the castle, she asked him how a man came to have such gold. He was so much in love that he told her, and showed her the purse, and when she asked, let her hold it—"

He paused for a moment, and the children, wide-eyed, leaned forward, rapt.

"Quick as a blink, she stepped inside and slammed the door in his face."

The children were loud with indignation.

"Before the mouth was out, Giovanni was out of the city with nothing but rags on his back, and the horn and the belt Guillametta had given him. He looked at the horn, and it looked like one they used in the army to summon soldiers.

"So he put it to his mouth and blew. Out of nowhere, soldiers dressed in blue and gold appeared before him. They saluted him and asked what his orders were. At his command, they surrounded the castle and demanded the princess give back the purse.

"Frightened, she brought it back and told him she had only jested at taking it. And she was so beautiful, and he was so foolish that she talked him into telling her about the horn, and then letting her hold it.

"No sooner was it in her hand than she blew it, and her orders to the soldiers were to take back the purse, give Giovanni a good beating, and throw him out of the city."

"What a fool," said a young boy, and Pietro nodded.

"In the evening," Pietro went on, "it grew cold, and he got angry and wished that he was wherever she had put the purse and horn—"

He looked about. A little girl piped up, "And he was!"

"So he was, in her very bedchamber, because she would not let them any farther from herself, and the princess was there, too. He snatched her by the waist and wished both of them to the end of the world. The princess begged and wept and lamented, but this time he was wise enough not believe. Still, she told him that he was tired, and he should sleep, and she would hold his head in her lap to show him how sorry she was. No sooner was he sleeping than she had the belt and the horn and the purse off of him, and wished herself back to her castle without him.

"His head fell to the hard earth, and he lamented his folly. At length. But—he was hungry, too. So he started walking, and he came to two apple trees, both covered with apples. One had all red apples, and one had all yellow ones. He was so hungry he gobbled down three red ones before he noticed that his nose was growing longer. And longer. It was three feet long before it stopped, and he was still hungry.

"So he ate a yellow apple, and his nose shrank a foot. And then he ate two more, and his nose was as it ever had been, and he was no longer hungry. Thinking they might be useful, he picked six red apples and six yellow apples, and walked on.

"The next day, those twelve apples were as ripe and fresh as they had been the day before, and he walked all the way back to the princess's kingdom, and they were still fresh. He was tattered and weathered and dusty, and he went to the castle and hawked his apples, his fine red apples fit for a princess.

"The princess wouldn't hear of anyone else having such fine apples. She came herself to buy them, with the purse of money, and carried them off to her balcony, where she gobbled them up, and her nose grew six feet long!

"Wasn't that a commotion in the land. The king offered her hand in marriage and half the kingdom to whoever could cure her, and the princess wept and wailed and wrung her hands, and did whatever the doctors told her, but her nose grew no shorter.

"But Giovanni took the money she had given him, and bathed and bought a fine green robe and a funny, foreign hat. He presented himself at the castle and said he had heard of such curses in his native land. The first sight of her with her nose six feet long cured him forever of loving her. But he took out the yellow apple and said it should cure her.

"She ate it, and her nose shrank by a foot. Everyone exclaimed in wonder, but Giovanni frowned, deep in thought. 'It should have cured her utterly,' he said. 'I must ponder why it failed. I have heard that sometimes it does not work as well if—if perchance the princess had something in her possession that does not rightfully belong to her.'

"'Oh, that,' said the princess, 'it was nothing important, I had just been joking.' She handed over the purse. He gave her another yellow apple, and her nose shrank again. He gravely said there was more, and for an apple each he got back the horn and the belt.

"Now, he would have given her the last two for nothing, but she thought, as she took the fourth, that she would reward him with death, not her hand, and gave him such a glare that he wished he was back with the pure and simple maiden Guillametta. And since he had the belt, back to the mill he went.

"They married, and they lived happily ever after, because once Guillametta heard the tale, she took the belt, the purse, and the horn, and the two yellow apples with them, and hid them away safely, so they would cause no more trouble."

"Ha!" said old Stephano. "Little boys and girls running off from home and school to go hunting for them! More trouble than they are worth!"

Laughter echoed all around.

"Not that it's been better for Orre," said Xenia. "First they went to this cousin, and he had this daughter who would never tell the truth, and never say anyone else was a liar, and no sooner than she had gotten cured and married, than she had a daughter who never laughs."

"True enough," sadi Pietro.

Only then did Alissandra notice the holes among the guests. A few children had left, and a few new married couples, but mostly the youths and the maidens—

Then, with a shriek, a mob burst upon them. Wearing rags and tatters, or clothes much too large for them, waving ragged flags, their faces covered with ash or charcoal, or a hood far too big, so that it hid the face entirely, and all of them shrieking and hollering and falling on the dishes to wave them in the air. . . .

Several frantic minutes later, when they all had vanished again, so had the bride and bridegroom.

"Whatever got into them?" said Pietro laughing. "You'd think they had better things to do—you'd best say and finish up the food—ah, you two—"

Alissandra glanced over. Two dark-haired children, a boy and a girl, were slipping back without having *quite* washed the charcoal off their faces. Her smile felt a little strained. At the court, the roisterers would be hirelings, like most of the entertainers, and still wear clothes more fine and fancy than here.

"You missed the fun," said Pietro, solemnly. "Roisterers broke in and made an uproar."

The girl giggled.

The boy said, "So tell us a story to make up for that." He pointed at Alissandra. "You tell us. About the card game. You said you would."

"Not if it takes too long," said Martin, the stable master at the Princess's Rest. "Got to get back to the stables."

"Baked for tomorrow already," said Alissandra, not quite keeping herself from sounding smug.

"King's coming," said Martin. "Just got the news—he's going hunting again."

Murmurs and nods came from all about, none showing great surprise, but Alissandra stood frozen, thinking of the pantry, comparing it to the castle's, pondering what pastries she could make—she could not beg Kate for help this soon.

Martin looked to be calculating grain and hay.

Bernardo laughed. "Don't frighten the lass too badly, Martin." He turned to her. "They hunt in the old style here, with hound and horn. They'd be ashamed to hunt in that new-fangled style with all the beasts driven before them—and he'd be ashamed to ask for fancy food at the inn."

"I will show how unfrightened I am," said Alissandra. "I will tell the tale! It is not, after all, long. Listen well! Once there was a lad, his name was Jack, and he went to the tavern to play cards. Luck was with him, and he won once, twice, thrice, until the man he played against said that his purse was empty, but he was King Marrack, and he had seven lovely daughters, and he'd bet letting Jack marry whichever one of them he pleased, if Jack put all the money he won against it.

"Jack agreed, and luck was still with him, so he won both the money and the leave, but before he did more than show his cards, the man vanished.

"So Jack got a pack of food and went walking, and wherever he went, he asked after King Marrack. No one had heard of him for leagues and leagues, but finally a little old woman who sold apples told him that he should go north to a lake, and stop by its shore, and he might learn something there.

"He went there and found it all surrounded by beech trees and rose bushes all in white flowers, and then, seven white swans flew out of the sky, landed in the lake, and swam up to the shore, where they took off their swan skins and were lovely maidens who went to bathe in the lake. Jack went over and took up one of those swan skins. The maidens ran for theirs and flew off as swans, except for the one who pled for him to give it back.

"'I will give it back,' said Jack, 'if you will tell me anything you know about King Marrack and where he lives.'

"She went very quiet at that but took back the swan skin and pointed out where seven hills stood. If he crossed them all, and seven times seven all told, through the wilderness, he would come to King Marrack's castle. And if he were wise, he would stay here in safety and never see that castle, for King Marrack was king over more than lands and men. She flew off, toward the hills, and he followed after and found King Marrack's castle."

"Like that?" said a small boy, scowling.

"Speedily a tale is spun," said Alissandra. "With less speed a deed is done. But he got there."

The small boy still looked disgruntled. She swept on.

"It was made all of gold, and when he drew near, swans flew over it and landed in the garden and turned to seven lovely maidens, those from the lake. Even though it had no fields or villages about it to be its kingdom.

"So he came up to the gate and knocked. King Marrack opened the door and gawked at him. 'What are you doing here?'

"'You did give me leave to marry one of your daughters,' said Jack. 'I came to woo one.'

"'I gave you no leave to come here,' said King Marrack. 'I won't have you wandering about my lands. You'll have to do three tasks for me to gain my leave to stay here and woo one. If you don't, I'll have your head for intruding, and you may sleep in the stables this night.'

"He lay down in the hay to sleep when the daughter who had told him how to come there came in, and she said, 'It was a rash promise I made, and I think you are the worse off for it, but I'll help. Tomorrow, he will tell you to chop up a whole stack of wood, and there will be two axes by it. One's all fine and sharp, the other all dull and rusty. Take the second to chop up the wood.'

"The next morning, King Marrack did as she said, and the dull axe looked so dull than he feared it would bounce off the wood and cut off his foot. He picked up the fine one, and hit a log with it, and it stuck to the next, instead of splitting, and a few more blows had fewer logs than when he started. So he took up the dull axe and cut this way and that, and all the wood fell apart into fine pieces before the hour was out, and the daughter came to him, and told him he would better have taken the second axe from the start—but they had all day and spent every hour talking, and he even learned her name was Serena.

"When evening came, King Marrack grumped and growled over every piece of wood, but he could find no fault in them. He said, 'I see you are a sly rogue, and my pity for your youth, setting you such an easy task, was misplaced. Tomorrow you will have a harder.'

"So Serena came to Jack that night, and told him that the next day her father would set him to empty out a well with a bucket, and he should use the bucket with holes, not the sound bucket. And so it was. When he tried the sound bucket, the well overflowed, but when he used the bucket with holes, it stopped with the first bucket-full, and was dry as a bone with the second. He and the daughter talked all day, and that evening King Marrack could find no fault except with his own lenience."

"He," said a little girl, her voice piping, and then fell silent, abashed, when they all looked at her.

"He what?" said Alissandra, mildly.

"He sounds like that ogre."

She shrugged. "There's only so many excuses you can make for when the man can do the deed—but that night, she warned him that he would break stones the next day, and to use the hammer with its head about to fly off its handle, not the well-put-together one. That one, when he tried it, made the rocks stick together, but the other one smashed them to gravel, and Jack and Serena could talk all day.

"That night, Serena came and said, 'He's not going to let you live tomorrow, he will chop your head off. We must flee at once. Take two horses from the stable, and the good axe, the good pail, and the good hammer.'

"They rode off before the night had far gone. They rode, and they rode, and in the morning, she said, 'My father will chase after us. If I look back at him, he will be able to curse us both. You must keep watch.'

"They rode on. Before the hour was out, he said, 'There is a great dust cloud behind us, and I can see your father in it.'

"She said, 'Let us ride past these trees.' And when they had, she had him take the good axe and, once her father had reached the trees, drive it into the nearest tree. So the trees grew larger and larger, and made a great forest, catching her father. Her father had to break free and go back to get the bad axe to cut them all down, and she and Jack rode on.

"And they rode and they rode, for hours, but then Jack saw the dust behind them again, and her father in it.

"She said, 'Let us ride through this valley.' And when they had, she had him take the good bucket and, once her father had reached the valley, upend it into the valley. It flooded the valley and bore off her father.

"She said that if her father were wise, he would go back, but if not, not. So they rode, and they rode, but her father went back and got the bad bucket to bail out the valley, and before the day was out, Jack saw the dust cloud, and it had her father in it.

"She said, 'Let us ride through this rocky pass.' And when they had, she had him take the hammer and, once her father had gotten into the pass, strike the rocks. The rocks all grew together, and that was the end of the pass, and of her father as well, so they rode to Jack's home, and married there, and lived well."

Alissandra drew a deep breath. There were smiles and nods all around. She sat and drank her cider. And they had been Jean's grandparents, which was how she knew the tale, but she would rather drink than talk now. She put the cup down and reached for the pitcher.

"Do you know more tales?" said a maiden.

"Not to tell without drinking more—and hearing more," said Alissandra.

"I fear that will be snatched from you," said Bernardo. She blinked and realized that he stood near the table, but not near his seat. "A prince is coming by, bringing his bride. And unlike the king's arrival, we have little time to prepare."

Lizina laughed and stood. "Easier than serving the princes every day."

The handful of inn servants, Alissandra among them, hurried down the dusty streets.

"A bride," grumbled Dora. "I hope this princeling doesn't think his wedding party will be greeted with flowers and festivities."

"Prince Hans," said Bernardo, "was reasonable enough when he came by here to Elferrin. Since he had the sense to reject Princess Esmeralda, we can have some hope for his bride."

Alissandra blinked. Prince Hans had recovered from his disappointment quickly. The thought struck her that he might have stumbled on Esmeralda, or Iolande, but did not last long.

"How many in his party?" she said. "And how many must I consider gentry?"

"Only the prince and his bride are high-born," Bernardo assured her. "Dozens at most for the party."

* * *

At the inn, she concluded she had enough of the fine white flour, and set to work. She might be here for a long time, she thought, as she stirred the bowl. Better off than Princess Aurelia, but not so well off as Serena, who married a good solid farmer.

She tested it. The dough was too sticky, and she added more flour. Then, she might marry one in the end, and not be in a tale, because she had nothing of that to tell about changing into a bird or escaping her evil father. Which was all to the good. And it would definitely be better than following Esmeralda about like a servant, to comb roses out of her hair.

She went to check the fire.

Chapter 7

The western sky still raged with scarlet and orange among a scattering of clouds, but the evening stars already shone clear above them. Along the road, men bore torches about the company, and the orange glow headed toward them.

Do not touch your hair to be certain, Alissandra told herself. You looked in the copper pot. It was burnished enough for you to be sure of how you looked. At any rate, Prince Hans and his bride will not care how the baker looks.

The younger girls giggled with excitement—a royal *bride*. The other maidservants were calm enough, merely carrying out the duty of greeting such high guests. Lizina must have mastered the art of appearing so calm at the castle; she could only hope that a princess's calm passed muster for a servant.

She supposed she was the only one wondering if she could curtsey like a proper servant. At least, she was hidden in the crowd, to muffle any awkwardness.

The torchmen, and a handful of riders, came up. Prince Hans threw his reins to a groom and dismount to help his bride down: a quiet young woman, with dark brown hair and a dark green dress. For a moment, as the prince took her hand, Alissandra blinked, but a second look only confirmed that the bride's hands were red and rough. She wondered what kitchen he had taken her from. The bridal couple came forward, and the maidservants curtsied like a field of flowers before a wind. Drab flowers, thought Alissandra, straightening, but at least she had not disgraced herself.

Their gazes went over her. The bride did not pick her out, but then, neither did Prince Hans. He really had thought only of Esmeralda, or else flour was an excellent disguise.

They went inside with the bowing Bernardo. She hurried back to the kitchen to ensure neither man nor cat meddled with the meat pastries.

With the pastries on the tray and conducted away, she looked at her hands. Better than a scullery maid's, at least. But then, princesses who rose again from the kitchen always seemed to have been scullery maids. Even Prince Hans's bride might be a princess.

She sighed. And began to calculate the rest of the baking.

* * *

Birds trilled sweetly outside. Uncommonly loud, thought Alissandra, burying her face in the pillow.

"Morning," said Lizina, firmly.

Alissandra groaned. She had thought she had mastered early rising, but her sleep had been wretched. She stirred herself to dress.

Before she finished slipping on her shoes, excited voices rose from below.

"Can you make them out?" said Lizina.

Alissandra shook her head. "From the courtyard, certainly."

They hurried down the stairs. In the middle of the courtyard stood a tree. A full grown apple tree, she thought, before she saw the glints among the leaves; it bore golden fruit, far too early for an apple tree.

"Pick one," said a stable boy. "I dare you."

She raised an eyebrow and looked him over. He snatched his hand out of sight, but not before she saw a bruise on it. Other boys giggled. She waved a hand loosely toward the nearest branch. The leaves drew back, swiftly, like a snail to the safety of its shell.

She turned away. "It looks as if they will have no fruit to their tarts, except from other trees."

A cascade of sweet laughter came from an upper window, where the bride looked down.

"Wait there," she called.

Moments, she walked into the courtyard, with a maid of middle years scurrying after, and told Alissandra to hold out her apron. She picked one fruit and put it down.

"No more than six," said Alissandra. "A pity for any to go to waste."

The bride nodded and picked all six. At this distance, the roughness and redness of her hands were blatant—a woman who spent hours scouring pots and pans. Still, even with the apron in her hands, Alissandra curtseyed as best she could.

"I will prepare them with all haste, Lady—" She froze. She should have caught that. There was no excuse for not knowing her name, and it would have been worse as a princess.

The maid sniffed. "Two-Eyes," she said.

* * *

The last peel fell to the board and glimmered, and she turned to chopping, and had them all in the bowl.

Two-Eyes, thought Alissandra as she reached for the jars. Not Helena or Talia—or even Kate. She mixed the sugar and cinnamon in. Nor the Beauty With Golden-hair, or Rose-Red, or even Catskins or Cap O'Rushes or All Kinds of Fur—or Parsley. Two Eyes.

The mix went into the tart easily, and she set it to bake, glad the ovens were stoked before she arose. She stepped to the door. Even in midsummer, it was cooler there, especially so early in the morning.

Two-Eyes's maidservant fluttered about the corner like a butterfly trying to move a horse. Two-Eyes herself kept her gaze on the inn maidservant she talked to, but she spoke too low voiced for Alissandra to hear.

The response was not so low. "O, she came here with her sister—or maybe it's her stepsister, they don't look much alike, but they don't talk—"

Two-Eyes spoke again.

"O we don't ask! That's the way to disaster. Ask strangers like that who they are and where they come from, and they turn out a pair of ladies. Best you can hope for is their storming off!"

Alissandra's eyebrows went up. Two-Eyes must have lived somewhere sheltered, not to know that. They could only hope that Prince Hans had her taught quickly, to ensure she offended no lord or lady at her firstborn's christening.

It hardly mattered. She have no wish to tell even Prince Hans the truth. She called over a stable boy, and told him to feed the apple cores and peelings to the prince's horse, or his bride's.

The boy cocked an eyebrow. "You're not curious."

"Not that curious," said Alissandra, firmly. She glanced at the doors. Travelers did not flow from the inn as they had on other mornings. They gathered about the tree and gawked. Some tried to snag a fruit, and sometimes the branches drew back, and sometimes they struck, even leaving the traveler sprawling the dust.

A few travelers seemed undeterred by that.

"Don't bother, don't bother," said one of Prince Hans's outriders. "No one but the lady can catch 'em."

One merchant, nursing his leg, his face set in malcontent lines, said, "You make her sound like a *lady* indeed."

The outrider shrugged. "There was this lord and this lady living in the forest between Elfarrin and Orre. You'd think they were peasants from their cottage, 'cept, *he* had only one eye, right dab in the middle of his forehead." He poked his own forehead to indicate where. The cook's little daughter and the head groom's little son giggled and poked their own foreheads. "And *she* had three, two like ordinary folks, and one like his. They had three daughters: one with one eye like him, one with two eyes like ordinary folks, one with three eyes like her, and instead of giving them pretty names, they called 'em One-Eye, Two-Eyes, and Three-Eyes."

Ah, thought Alissandra

"And they hated Two-Eyes, they did. They made her do all the work, and gave her only burnt and broken bits to eat, because she only had two eyes, like ordinary folk."

"But—but—" sputtered a drover. "Don't most lords and ladies have two eyes?"

"Goes to show how ordinary they are," said the outrider. "But one day, a goat got into their garden where they grew their herbs, and munched away, so with much hooting and hollering, they got it out again, and cuffed Two-Eyes for not stopping it, and sent her to take the goat to pasture.

"She took 'em, and the goat said to her, They treat you mighty bad here, but I'll be your friend. Pull on my horn, and it'll come off.

"So it did, and it was all full of food. All day long, the goat ate, and so did Two-Eyes. In the evening, she put the horn back on and led them back. Lasted for weeks, but then One-Eye and Three-Eyes told their parents that Two-Eyes wasn't eating the scraps and crusts they left her, and she was still plumper than ever.

"They set One-Eye to watch her, and One-Eye came out to the pasture. Two-Eyes invited her to sit and then sang a lullaby—One-Eye, are you waking? One-Eye, are you sleeping?—until she slept. The goat and Two-Eyes could eat in peace, but One-Eye had to tell her parents she had seen nothing.

"They set Three-Eyes the next day. Two-Eyes sang a lullaby again, but she made a mistake—she sang, Three-Eyes, are you waking? Two-Eyes, are you sleeping? Two of Three-Eyes's eyes went to sleep, but the third stayed awake, and watched. She told her parents what she had seen, and that very night, her parents went to slaughter the goat. Weeping, Two-Eyes ran and told the goat, who said that it could not be stopped, but she was to eat none of its flesh, only beg its bones and skin, and bury them together.

"So while they feasted on the goat, she dug the grave and wept over it, and the next day, where the grave was—"

He gestured at the tree.

"Full-grown overnight, it was. And none of *them* could pick any of the apples—only Two-Eyes.

"They didn't treat her any better for that, and when Prince Hans was separated from his men , and rode up to ask directions, they hid her under a wash tub. But he had eyes only for the tree, and begged for a fruit. One-Eye and Three-Eyes tried to magic it down, but that was no good. And Two-Eyes had picked an apple earlier, and she rolled it to him. He found her under the wash tub, and she picked him all the apples he could wish for.

"He liked her a lot, she was so pretty, and brought her away with him, and when they stayed the night, the tree grew in the courtyard of the inn."

From the doorway, Bernardo harumphed. "I had a tree stuck in the middle of my courtyard until *tonight*?"

"It'll leave then," another of Prince Hans's men said, quickly.

Bernardo harumphed again and went back in.

Alissandra let out her breath and went back in herself to check the tarts.

As she pulled them out, Bernardo was outside the door, instructing a stable boy to tell the villagers that if they wanted to have a mug of ale and see that marvelous tree, they had best do it soon. For a moment her mouth twitched. Then she considered whether they would have a bit of bread and cheese with it, and on her first day alone in the bakery, at it.

* * *

Alissandra made her curtsey with the other servants giving a royal farewell, and then stood to watch them leave. Songbirds seemed to sing about the bridal couple with uncommon numbers. Then, Two-Eyes was a lady, even if one put upon by her family.

But the bread was baking. She turned to go in.

"Luckier than the other one," said a groom.

"What?" said Alissandra.

"The other prince that wooed Princess Esmeralda," said—Ned, she thought.

"There were two others. Prince Ivan and Prince John."

"Well," said Ned slowly, "I don't know nothing about Prince Ivan—"

"Got safely home," said another groom—Gian. "Crowned and all. King Ivan now."

"Eh, then he's all right," said Ned. "It was Prince John who's worse off."

"What?" said Alissandra. "Did he rescue Princess Esmeralda?"

Gian's laugh was a short bark.

Ned looked sober. "No. There was this lady—an old crone, she lived alone in the woods. She made a pot of soup, and it was too hot, so she went and put it in the stream to cool it. Right in the ford where there were rocks to hold it up. Except that Prince John came to ford the stream. Broke the pot, spilled the soup, got cursed that he will never marry unless he finds Anthousa Xanthousa Chrismalousa." Ned shook his head. "Went home to tell his parents and went off the next day to find her."

Her mouth pursed. She could only hope that this Anthousa Xanthousa Chrismalousa proved a better bride than Esmeralda.

"At least the king won't come today," said Gian, cheerfully. "Prince Hans—and her—are going that way. He'll have to greet them and have them as guests."

"Tomorrow, on the other hand," said Ned, grimly.

* * *

The clouds were soft but dark. Rumbling thunder echoed. And it rained.

And rained.

Which meant, thought Alissandra, no hunting. (And the king had had to put off the hunt, she heard, to deal with problems.) But it affected nothing else, it seemed. Except the travellers' moods. Sullen drovers, merchants, pilgrims, messengers, and all the rest filtered into the inn.

She molded the latest loaf of bread. And wondered what it would be like in the winter. No doubt she would learn from experience.

Lizina came into the kitchen. "Have they told you of the hay dances? Three of them, after the haying. Apparently fine feathers are expected."

Alissandra opened her mouth to say that was a long time off yet, realized how little time she had to sew each day, and said, "Did they tell you where one might buy cloth?"

She didn't have a loom, she didn't have a spinning wheel, but she could sew. Here, no one but her had any concern for her wardrobe.

"They did just happen to mention that old Annabella might have some becoming shades. Dyed in the wool, no less." Lizina glanced at the dough. "Will you have some free time?"

"This is the last batch," Alissandra said, and started to ready the loaves. "As soon as they bake."

* * *

Days turned into weeks. The blue cloth turned into a gown, and thoughts of how, at the castle, the cloth would have been finer, the dye brighter, the skirt fuller, and the whole thing decked with embroidered flowers, were only twinges, especially as time passed. Her fingers regained their callouses from sewing, though she had to make the sleeves larger, with all the work she did kneading dough. Who knew? Some youths might still fear her as a lady, appearing so mysteriously, enough to be no more than polite and distant. Others might be bold enough to woo her. Her mouth twitched. Then she might be abducted, or turned into a bird, to be rescued. Such things could happen even to peasant girls.

One day, she noticed her feet no longer ached after hours of standing. She could not have told when it changed.

Then a boy careened into the kitchens as she brought out the bread. "The ale, the best ale—"

"Whatever happened to *you*?" said the cook, waving a ladle.

"The king is here!"

A murmur of consternation ran about. One undercook said, "King Matteo? Without even a hour's warning?" and another said, "This late?"

Lizina, by the window, said, "He must have taken a fast horse. The laundry's done, I'll fetch the ale."

"And I'll fetch the bread and butter," said Alissandra.

"Honey, too," said the cook.

"He's got lots of men," said the boy, diverting the kitchen maids before she left. She had the tray ready and back moments before Lizina returned with the ale.

"Now we shall see how truthfully the rumor talked," murmured Alissandra. Lizina smiled. Alissandra considered the tray and her curtsey. A glance at the windows showed that the western sky was turning pink. Late indeed, like any commonplace traveler.

She managed the curtsey well enough and straightened to look, and think how young he was. Brown-haired, green-eyed, a grave expression that could not completely hide that he might be younger than she was.

Then, thought Alissandra, there's been no talk of a queen yet. Bernardo took the tray, but the king's gaze went from her to Lizina and back.

"Is this the new baker who made tarts of golden apples?"

Alissandra curtseyed. "I could make venison pastries of a snow-white stag, as well, but it would take longer. First you would have to avoid letting it lead you to a witch."

King Matteo laughed, a surprised bark. For a moment, he looked almost merry. "Your skills will not be put to such a test. Not yet. I will hunt deer before they eat half the harvest, but now—" He shook his head, and looked grim. "I have more urgent matters. We must rest this night and rouse at dawn."

Lizina curtseyed. Alissandra did the same, and then followed her from the room. Lizina went upstairs, and Alissandra returned to the kitchen, to find it sibilant with tales of a robber band.

"I don't know how the king got wind of them so soon," said the scullery maid Rosa.

"Seven leagues boots, perhaps," said Alissandra, smiled at the laughter, and went to fetch the bread.

* * *

That evening, Nora pulled the spoon from the stew and let it steam. "So now you've seen our king."

"So I have," said Alissandra.

Nora snorted. "Well, that's the one we're left with. You should have seen his younger brother. Prince Giovanni. Now there was a young man who made every eye turn. Golden and gorgeous and great-hearted. Even his older brother—Prince Sandrino—was more regal and grave, like a king should be. But this one! Stuck with the middle one!"

Half the kitchen smiled as if they had heard her often before.

"I've heard of times where the older two—girls—had to go off in a coach and six with no further ado, and the youngest with a black bull, to a lot of trouble, but never one where the older ones got to be queens while the youngest did not."

Not true, thought Alissandra.

Nora turned to her. "Have you ever heard of such a thing?"

"Two Eyes," said Alissandra.

Silence fell.

"Two Eyes was a middle daughter."

A skitter of laughter ran through the kitchen.

Nora pouted. "Ladies and lords are odd things. Have you ever heard such a thing among royalty?"

Alissandra smiled, coolly. "Not that I will tell you if you don't tell me about the king."

Laughter resounded. Nora looked indignant, and the old cellarer Tomas wiped his eyes and began.

"Our king and queen had three sons, like she said. Sandrino was his father's favorite, Giovanni, his mother's—and Matteo's, his grandparents', but they died, making their son king, when the princes were near grown. Soon after, there was a great wild boar in the woods, tearing up trees and travelers, destroying crops and orchards and cottages.

"The king said that whichever son killed the boar would be his heir, so all three set out and split up in the woods. Giovanni tracked it down and killed it. He took its head and hide and started back when Sandrino found him." Tomas shook his head. "He killed him, threw his body in the river, and returned with the head and hide. He told Matteo he had not seen Giovanni, but when Matteo hunted for Giovanni he did not find him—or the body.

"But one day, a wandering shepherd picked a reed from the riverbank to make a pipe, and he played merrily on it. When the court came out to hunt, he was summoned to play for them.

"No sooner had he lifted the pipe before the royal court than it would play no merry tunes. It only sang, 'I slew the boar, and my brother slew me. The older brother did the deed. The middle brother did me no harm.'"

Grim faces and nods were all around the kitchen. Alissandra swallowed and wondered how many of them had been there.

"Wasn't that an uproar. Matteo asked where the reed had grown, and went there, to have the body dug up, and they found it at once. Could know from the rings.

"Nothing more for it then. They buried Giovanni, and cut off Sandrino's head, and between the queen's grieving for Giovanni and the king's for Sandrino, both were dead within a year. So we have King Matteo."

"For," said Nora, "not killing the boar."

"Or the brother," said Tomas.

"There are kings and queens who did less for the throne," said Alissandra. "My parents—" She hesitated. Then—"My parents always said that tales were miserable things, and our king and queen should be glad not to be any. As glad as those sisters you spoke of—" She nodded to Nora. "Who went off in a coach-and-six."

Nora cackled. "You came from Elfarran? Well, they are in one now!"

Alissandra smiled coolly.

"And one they would be better out of," said Rosa, with feeling.

"It's enough," said the kitchen maid Zizi, "to make you glad we have only dances, not balls."

"And," said Alissandra, "that the king doesn't invite us all to a ball as a challenge to a master thief."

Laughter resounded. "Oh, yes, that would be dreadful, better a dance—"

The talk turned to the harvest ball with no more thought of the king, and all the kitchen maids converged on Lizina and Alissandra to assure them about what preparations they needed. Even Finella, even after Nora pointed out, sharply, to her that she was too young.

* * *

Lizina and Alissandra lugged a basket of flowers between them, filled with wheat snow—not the blooms in white or cream-color from which they drew their name, but shades of pink and blue. Other maids, laughing and chattering of the dance, were carrying other flowers, mostly red and orange hay flame, but that color would hardly become them.

Alissandra stepped on a stone, it slipped under the foot, and she staggered, nearly falling. "I could have combed my hair and washed my hands," she grumbled.

"And been the center of the dance," said Lizina, softly. "Everyone would ask where you got those flowers, out of season."

Alissandra let her breath out. True. No one would ask after them, but there was no such fear of asking where flowers came from.

"Hurry!" called Zizi the kitchen girl. "You haven't got long." She scurried off with her own flowers, with Rosa with her. Since they would need two sets of hands to array them.

Lizina and Alissandra started up the stairs.

"I wonder," said Alissandra, "whether arriving late is proper. Midnight, say."

"That's only for balls," said Lizina.

"Where people don't have to rouse in the morning," said Alissandra, wearily. "But if I stayed up to midnight, I would stay up all night. I would be groggier for the few hours' sleep."

In their room, they dressed and set about doing their hair. Sorting out the becoming colors, the paler to Lizina and the stronger to her was simple enough, but after it, Alissandra bit her lip. There was more of an art to it than she realized, in putting flowers in their hair.

"It's considered lucky to have the dance floor strewn with flowers by the end of the dance," said Lizina.

"How lucky for me," said Alissandra.

When they finally descended, Alissandra glanced at her reflection in the great copper pot, burnished to a ruddy mirror, and concluded she was at least presentable.

"Come, come," called Zizi. Her black hair and Rosa's nut-brown were aflame with the flowers. "You've never been to the dance."

"They might have been to others," said Nora, in reproof.

Zizi opened her mouth and clapped her hands to it, as if just remembering how dangerous it was to ask.

"Off with you then," said Nora, but even as they walked to the door, Alissandra could hear the noise outside. Outside, the courtyard held a crowd, and even the servants dressed for the dance did not move off.

She had to edge through the crowd to see the young couple at its center: a handsome young man, richly dressed in clothes rather the worse for wear, and a bashful young servant maid, rather pretty.

"Wasn't she here before?" said a groom.

"Yes," said another. "She was with the family, the ones we heard of, that the robbers got."

Alissandra blinked. So the news of the robbers had reached them.

"I escaped," said the maid. Silence spread so quickly that Alissandra wondered that it had been so noisy before. The maid faltered, and her gaze went down. The young man murmured to her, and she straightened, a little.

Zizi seized her hands, and Lizina's, and whispered, "They'll want to know at the dance."

And, though Alissandra, she wanted to know herself.

"All the family died," said the maid, hesitantly. "Torn to pieces. But I rolled to bushes when first they attacked, and they did not mark me. And when they left, I was lost in the woods." She swallowed. "But a little white dove brought me a key, and showed me a tree with a door in it. It held food, and a bed and fire. After a few days, the dove asked me to go to a hut of an old woman and, without speaking to her, fetch a ring in her hut, the one that was quite plain.

"The old woman made quite a pother about how rude it was to go in without speaking to her, and there were—o, so many rings! But I found it, and went back to the dove, except the dove was gone. I leaned back against a tree—"

Her head went down again, and she blushed rosy red.

The man laughed. "And my branches came to be arms about her. And now we return to my father's kingdom."

"Not at once," said Bernardo. "King Matteo will want to hear of this witch."

"Not the robbers?" said the man.

"He's heard of the robbers. But the road will be easy after. This is the Princess's Rest, where seven roads converge."

Zizi, bright-eyed, started to tug Alissandra away, toward the dance.

* * *

She thought they went as swiftly as feet could carry a person, toward the dance, but the great barn was already abuzz with the tale of the servant girl and the tree prince. Zizi and Rosa, surrounded by swarms of listeners, added what details she could before the music began.

With that, they were all off in a great circling dance of youths and maidens, until, flushed and out of breath, they finished the measure.

Only, Alissandra discovered, for another youth to claim her for another dance.

And another, and another. At the end of the fourth, Alissandra saw Lizina watching, and wondered whether she could, perhaps, decline a few dances despite her governess's strictures. She would not terminally offend a prince or an ambassador if she did; she certainly would not provoke a war.

Another man already approached her. "Come and eat," he said, smiling.

Relieved, she joined him in the throng eating honey cakes and ripe peaches, and gabbling about the serving maid.

"Lucky thing that robber captain didn't come a-wooing," said Rosa. "We might be having a wedding now only for the bride to declare she'd gone to the woods after him—except she'd say she was only dreaming, and her bridegroom would say, it wasn't so, and God forbid it should be so—and in his lair, she'd seen him and his band tearing some poor woman to pieces and *eating* her." She spread her hands. "And then she pull out the dead woman's finger, and we'd have to go hunt the band down."

"And God forbid it should be so!" called the young farmer Will, and everyone laughed about them.

Alissandra managed only a smile. How that tale had given her nightmares when she was young—"Much better to leave it in the king's hands."

Rosa nodded. "And beware of strange wooers!"

"Your cousin Teresa isn't listening to that," said Belinda, spitefully. At Alissandra's glance, she waved at where a brown-haired lass clung to the arm of a young man looking at her with possessive pride.

"Ah, that's Jean," said Rosa. "Just because he went for a soldier doesn't mean he's a stranger." She looked about. "Now, *she's* a stranger." Another woman, with red-gold hair, looked wistfully about. "Old Ivo hired her, but no one knows her."

"Eulalie," said a youth, brightly. "Her name's Eulalie."

Alissandra's mouth twitched. She could not remember his name, but he lived by Old Ivo's farm.

"A tale," called Zizi. "A tale before another dance, since Alissandra Baker says she's heard of a middle child like our own King Matteo—and that Two-Eyes."

"What?" said Lizina. "Telling you the tale of the mangy man was not enough to satiate you forever?"

Laughter and cries of "No!" arose. Alissandra lifted her eyebrows and shifted her way out of the crowd, to where the musicians played.

"Once upon a time," she declaimed, "a queen was married and had a son. Then her husband died, and she married again, and when that husband died, she married yet again. That time, she choose badly, and her husband was cruel and lorded it over her and all the kingdom, and soon grief killed her."

"I thought it was about a middle prince," said Zizi.

"Hush, child," said Rosa. "Let her tell it!"

"Her third husband called himself regent and made many new laws. One was about a tree that grew by the royal castle and bore golden apples. It had been law that anyone could pick one, but the new regent declared that anyone who so much as touched that tree would die for it, and set guards all about to enforce it.

"But every year, just as the fruit ripened, it vanished, all in a night. The guards fled the regent's wrath in the morning, but they told enough that everyone heard that they had fallen magically asleep. The regent set guards on the guards, and then guards on the guards of the guards, but every year, he had only fled guards and a fruitless tree.

"The seventh year, a clever old huntsman came and told the regent he could catch the thief. So he set the tree all about with crafty nets, even in the branches, and when the morning came, the nets held a great golden bird, and the regent had it put in a cage.

"Now the young prince was playing one day in the courtyard. He had a toy sword of wood, and the regent had uttered dire threats if ever he lost it. That day, the sword slipped loose and fell into the cage, and though the prince tried and tried, he could not draw it out. So he stole the keys to the cage, and when he thought the bird asleep, he tried to sneak in to gain the sword. But the bird flew out at once.

"And when it had flown, the prince found that it had turned his hair gold, and the sword steel, and on the sword was written, Call upon the golden bird to win battles. He wrapped up his hair in a cap that covered it all, and headed to the road that led most quickly out of the kingdom.

"In the next kingdom, he went to the castle and asked for a post. They hired him to help the gardener. So he hid the sword in his hut and spent his days planting and digging and weeding, and every day, he had to pick three nosegays of flowers and bring them for the three princesses.

"One day, it was so hot in the sun that he took off his cap when he was alone in the garden, but the middle princess saw how his hair gleamed from a high window. The next morning, she rose up early in the morning, before the dew dried, so as to be there when he came with the nosegays. She said that it was not proper for him to wear his hat in her presence. He bowed and said he must, because he had a sore on his head, and she tried to snatch the cap away, and he escaped with it, but not before she had glimpsed the gold again.

"That very day, the king proclaimed that he wished to know which of his councilors was the wisest. Whoever set a riddle that one and only one of his councilors could answer would be rewarded with a purse of pearls, a purse of gold, and a purse of silver.

"The gardener's boy picked three peaches, one over-ripe, one just ripe, and one still green, and joined those who asked their riddles. When it was his turn, he gave the overripe peach to the oldest princess, the just ripe one to the middle princess, and the green one to the youngest princess. Only one councilor could explain the meaning of this to the king.

"'Your Majesty, what this means is that your oldest daughter has long been ready to marry, your middle daughter is just ready to marry, and your youngest daughter is not ready yet.' Which pleased the king, both because he knew which of his councilors was the wisest, and because he could now see that he had neglected his daughters.

"He gave orders then, and in a month and a day, the young men of the kingdom, the knights and the nobles, thronged the court, that the princesses might choose their bridegrooms. The elder princess came among them with a golden cup, and whoever she gave the cup to, was to be her bridegroom. She walked across the hall and gave the cup to a high-born nobleman, and all hailed her choice.

"And came the middle sister out, she too with a cup, but she walked among all the noblemen and knights, down every row, and gave the cup to no man, and said that she had not seen her bridegroom among them.

"So the king summoned up all the young men who were merchants and tradesmen and farmers, and in a month and a day, the middle princess walked among them, and gave the cup to no man, and said that she had not seen her bridegroom among them.

"So the king summoned up all the young men who were peasants and herdsmen and servants, and as soon as she saw the gardener's boy, she gave him her cup.

"The king wanted to bring him to the castle, but the gardener's boy feared they would see his hair, so he said he was a gardener's boy when the princess choose to marry him, so a gardener's boy he would remain.

"As they readied for the weddings, the gardener's boy's stepfather sent word that the golden bird had been seen in the king's kingdom, and they must have lured it there. If they did not send him it at once, he would declare war. Since no one had seen the bird, they readied themselves for war. The king made the nobleman his oldest daughter would marry into a general, and the nobleman offered the gardener's boy an old nag to ride if he wanted to go to war.

"So the gardener's boy mounted this nag, took his sword, rode out until he was all alone. Then he unsheathed the sword and called upon the bird. At once there appeared seven score knights, all mounted on red horses and wearing red armor, and they brought him a magnificent red steed and magnificent red armor. He armed himself, and they rode after the army, which they found sore pressed. The gardener's boy led his knights to the attack, and they routed the army of his stepfather. Then he rode off again, and called upon the bird, and so the knights left with the horse and the armor, and he rode back on the old nag.

"The noblemen jeered at him, saying that even if he could not fight, he had missed a sight, with the great noble who had appeared by magic and his noble knights.

"But a soldier of the stepfather had seen the gardener's boy's golden hair, and so the stepfather declared that they were harboring his treacherous and ungrateful stepson, and therefore attacked again.

"The nobleman led out the army again, and gave the gardener's boy the old nag, and this time, the golden bird gave him knights in green armor on black horses, and for himself magnificent green armor and a magnificent black steed, and once again routed his stepfather.

"The stepfather feigned contrition and spoke of signing a peace treaty. The king feared treachery, and brought his army with him, led by the nobleman. The stepfather attacked. The gardener's boy followed, wearing magnificent golden armor and riding a magnificent golden steed, leading seven score knights, and though the king nearly died, the gardener's boy hacked through his enemies and saved his life, though he suffered a wound to his leg in the time. The king himself bound up the wound, and with his own handkerchief, and the gardener's boy rode off as soon as the fighting was done.

"He returned to the castle, himself limping as badly as the nag, and the middle princess saw him go to his hut.

"When the king returned, lamenting that he could not discover who his rescuer was, the middle princess told him she could show him. She led him to the hut where the gardener's boy lay, and they saw the king's handkerchief on his leg wound. Then she pulled off his cap and showed his golden hair.

"Then the king begged him to tell them who he was, who had delivered the realm, and whose forces had slain the evil regent of the next kingdom.

"So, with his stepfather dead, he told him who he was. Therefore, the oldest princess married the nobleman, and the middle princess married the prince, and he took her back to his kingdom, where they were crowned king and queen, and reigned for many a year, and held to the old law, that anyone who wanted to pick a golden apple might do so."

Zizi scowled. "How did the stepfather know the prince had golden hair if he ran away?"

"A servant saw him," said Alissandra. "Before he got away."

Jean put down his mug. "This is a dance. Is everyone too weary to dance at it?"

Roars of denial went up, and calls for the musicians to play the hare's ring. Alissandra's eyebrows went up, but she joined in the measures and wild exchanges about the ring, so fast that at the end of the dance, all the dancers fell out, calling for water and fighting to catch their breath. Not the dance to call for if you wanted to keep dancing, thought Alissandra, drinking with the rest.

The strange woman—Eulalie, was it?—spoke with the panting musicians, stepped where Alissandra had told her tale, and began to sing. Such a sweet voice, Alissandra thought, and all about, dancers grew quiet to hear her singing.

About how a soldier had been lost in the woods and come to an ogre's house. How the ogre had set him impossible tasks, but the ogre's daughter had helped him—and then, when her father decided to kill him, task or no task, helped him to flee, and they had pledged each other, but how, when he returned to his own village, a woman had bewitched him to forget the daughter—

At that, Jean, who had listened standing still as a post, shook off Teresa's hand—Alissandra realized that Teresa had tried to pull him out of the dance—and strode up to Eulalie to kiss her and stop her song.

"It's not true!" shouted Teresa. "It's not true! *She* bewitched him! Just now! You heard her, with the song...."

A man grabbed her arm, and Alissandra remembered he was one of the boundsmen. His tasks included arresting criminals. Other men came to help him, and still others went off to search her cottage. Alissandra pulled back against the wall to avoid being in the way, putting her in the thick of those exclaiming over the story. And tell how they had always known Teresa was trouble. Or declare it was good that the king had gone to deal with bandits, since when he returned, he could deal with a witch as well.

Zizi murmured, to her and Lizina, "I supposed we don't have to *ask* where Eulalie came from."

Said Lizina, mildly, "There's many a good bride—even a good queen—who was an ogre's daughter."

* * *

That night, as she prepared for bed, Alissandra stopped to open the box where she had stored the feathers, and look at them.

"Ready to call on them for knights?" said Lizina.

"They didn't come with a promise," said Alissandra, wearily. "And—whom would they fight?" She sighed and closed the box.

Chapter 8

Late summer rolled on.

King Matteo, returning from putting down the bandits, made the prince and his bride welcome, and judged Teresa.

And summer rolled into fall.

Once, as the leaves turned the hills into gold and scarlet, Alissandra looked over them and saw, not a skein of geese flying south, but a wedge of swans, carrying a carpet, and a person on it. She watched them go until they vanished from sight, and turned back to her baking.

Having baked the wedding cake, she attended Jean and Eulalie's wedding with all the rest.

Day after day, travelers came without tales, and she baked and baked and baked and baked. Lizina gathered linens and washed them white. Belinda no longer brought the meat from the butcher; her brother came instead, and gossips tittered about the folly of her trying to trap Bernardo.

King Matteo did come to hunt in the forest, more than once. She made the fine white bread when she had warning enough of the visit—often enough—huntsmen would come to look for where the deer ran—and heard the chatter about how he hunted often this year. Though, they conceded, the deer had been plentiful.

"There's many a peasant who'll be pleased with his crop next year, with the deer thinned out."

And sometimes they talked of how it showed hardiness, hunting in the old style, chasing the deer with hounds.

"Not like those kingdoms where the huntsmen chase all the deer together so the king can shoot thirty in a shot."

Or the king did not hunt at all, thought Alissandra, lugging water. Her father did not.

Once such night, Alissandra laid down the bread by the stew, for the dinners, and went to leave again.

Nora looked up from the stew pot. "He should be hunting a bride. Both brothers dead, and all his father's sisters married off in foreign lands—he should wed and raise up an heir."

"True," said Rosa, "we might end up like Orre."

"And the problem there?" said Alissandra. They all looked at her. "They had a queen with a nose magically enormous, who never wed. So they ended up with her distant cousin. What's to be said about that? They got a princess who was always telling stories, and would never call anything a story—but they got her to say it in the end, and married her off. And her daughter, the worst they could say of her is that she never laughed. It's not like their queen would have had children any better."

After a moment of silence, in which Finella scowled, Zizi said, "Perhaps he's hunting a doe that turned into a woman."

Looks of horror spread across the taproom, even on the faces of foreign travelers.

"Perhaps," said a foreign merchant, "the hind is leading him to a grave where a dove will tell him one of his men-servants is a lady and a widow—'cause the bird's a ghost of the dead husband—and he'll execute her mother for killing her husband, and then marry her."

"Worse things can happen," said Alissandra, dryly. At least they had no chance that King Matteo would go looking for Esmeralda and Iolande. "But that time, the hind led him to the grave at once."

Zizi shrugged. "Sometimes it happens differently."

"People could vanish in the wood, because of some cursed wildman," said a traveler. "Even kings, I've heard of tales like that. Next thing you know, the heir's been promised to the wildman, and then what's the point?"

* * *

One day when snowflakes stung like bees in the sharp wind, Bernardo, smiling jovially, appeared in the bakery door, and was followed by a girl a few years younger than Alissandra, with nut-brown hair and bright eyes, shifting from foot to foot in excitement.

"With winter travelers being few and far between," said Bernardo, "it's a good season to take a prentice and teach her to bake. Then when the summer throngs return, two sets of hands will make sure there is bread enough for all."

The girl looked anxiously at her.

"Her name is Carla."

Alissandra nodded gravely. The girl had not come from the village—but she could no more ask Carla than Carla could ask her where she came from.

"I'm about to bake another batch," she said, and stood aside to let Carla in.

She gave the girl a sidelong glance. One couldn't tell, after all. She would not have taken Two Eyes for a lady, herself, and at least Carla's hands were clean.

* * *

In the evening, by candlelight, Lizina undressed in their room, and observed, "Carla brought a bundle. Cloth by its weight, but she stashed it away like a treasure."

Alissandra stood up, not glancing at her own box. "Worse than wondering," she said cheerily. "To have such a clue."

Lizina chuckled. "Perhaps it will explain something else."

"Who has guessed about us, yet?"

"Everyone," said Lizina. "No one is right."

Alissandra sighed. That was true. And most of them guessed that she and Lizina were twins.

She crawled into bed, under the heaped blankets. The wind gusted, rattling the chimney. Snow hissed from the roof, and she sighed.

* * *

A late snowfall melted into the ground without perturbing the crocuses in their delicate blues and creams. Alissandra sighed. Spring mud and spring floods hindered travelers, if not like winter snows, but summer was coming. Dusty summer, but easier for travel.

Then she saw the outriders.

"King's coming," she said.

Carla looked down at her floury hands and front. "You'll have to—"

Alissandra laughed. "I saw the outriders. You have time."

And indeed, Carla appeared beside her, ready to curtsey when the royal party arrived, and Alissandra counted off the ranks of those with him. Then she kept Carla with her as she returned to count out loaves.

"All the bread?" said Carla.

"More," said Alissandra, adding pieces. "I counted the nobles. Every loaf we made will give each of them a mouthful."

She handed Carla one tray, and took up the other to lead the way out. Lizina, lugging laundry the other way, lifted her eyebrows and stepped aside to let them pass.

The upper room was filled with nobles, and many of them foolishly clad if they meant to hunt.

"Ah, the bakers with hair like ripe wheat, and the good earth it springs from!" said King Matteo.

Alissandra dipped a little, as well as she could with her hands full.

"White bread?" A nobleman—not one who had hunted with King Matteo before—looked at it. "Are we not hunters? Are we dainty courtiers?"

Alissandra straightened. "The white bread keeps better," she said, tartly. "For your return, I can make you as much brown bread as you desire, but for now you have to content yourself with what keeps. Unless you're too dainty for it."

To her surprise, laughter resounded, as if at some great jest. Silently, wondering what was that funny, she curtseyed with Carla to leave.

* * *

On a summer day, with brown, coarse loaves stacked for travelers or returning hunters, Alissandra left the bakery and passed through the taproom, toward the door.

"Hunts a lot," said one grizzled drinker, and took another swig of
ale.

"There's been a lot of deer," said one young man, mildly. "Would eat
us out of hearth and home, if they weren't hunted."

An old woman, nursing her drink by the fireplace, hooted with
laughter. "You're out for venison, I know you, young man."

He blushed fiery red, and laughter boomed.

The grizzled man muttered over his drink. "Like kings have to be
careful with their duties."

"Since the boar, yes," said Tomas, marking off tallies and going to fill
mugs with more ale. "Very conscientious about hunting."

"Not like now," said the grizzled man. "not last year even. Mark my
words, he's looking for prey on two legs."

One started to speculate about how he had found a castle and wok-
en an enchanted lady who had slept there for a hundred years, and now
he visited her and his children.

"Whatever for? It's not like his mother could try to serve them up
to him for dinner, however lowly the bride was by birth."

Alissandra walked past, out into the summer sunshine. No travelers
quite yet. No sign of the hunting party returning, of course.

He could give a ball, of course. She had not brought ballgowns, but
perhaps she was not the only princess drudging away in a hot kitchen
in the kingdom.

Birds flitted by. And if she drudged forever, it would make it into
no tale.

She sighed. Perhaps Carla would unwrap her gowns and win herself
the king.

* * *

It was Tomas who first said, as the sunshine turned orange with evening, that the hunt was late. There was laughter and suggestions that they must have found fine hunting—or poor hunting, which was why no carcasses had been sent to be roasted—but despite the unease in both, Alissandra had not thought much of it, even when it spread to the stable boys.

When the clouds in the west blazed with scarlet and flame, everyone said it, with gravity or worry or terror. Some muttered about wild men of the woods who saw to it that anyone who went into their forests never came out again. This time, they sounded more like a warning than repeating an old tale.

Bernardo roared with laughter at that, and pointed out those wild men never let any beast escape alive, either. That did not assure Alissandra. It might be a different sort of wild man. Or a witch instead. Or something worse. She retreated to the bakery, to find Carla flitting uselessly about, her hands clutching at air as if she could accomplish something.

"We will start tomorrow's bread." Her voice was flat and heavy.

To measure, to mix, to knead, to set aside, only took so much time. Alissandra looked banefully at the dough, which would not encourage it to rise any more swiftly. She had to await its own good time. She left.

Outside, in the still hot gloom, lights shone from the inn and about houses. Here and there, she could pick out, by that light, a snatch of wall, a stand of trees, wildflowers in a ditch. Clumps of people gathered and talked in low voices of every forest peril of every tale, and uselessly, of searching.

Alissandra walked on. Dew already formed on the grass, and wet the edge of her skirt. She looked over the fields again, where wheat spread, and trees were vague with distance. No breeze made wheat bend, or boughs shift, but *something* moved. Her breath caught. She forced it out, and watched. They did not need for the baker to send them all chasing after something blown by the wind. She took a step forward. The stray light showed more clearly: a rider, his head hanging, coming over a field. A horse weary beyond belief, plodding along.

"Who are you?" she called. Silence fell behind her, and she could feel the gazes behind her. "Do you need aid?"

For a moment, she thought that head would rise, but it did not. The horse moved no more swiftly. Still, she could make out, vaguely, a noble who had joined the hunt.

Men ran past her. One took the horse's bridle. Others took down the rider and carried him on.

Alissandra ran back to the inn. "One's back," she called. Stable boys gawked at her. "*You* have to look to his horse, it's half-dead—but he looks like death, himself. We need—" Her hand plucked at air. "Do we have broth?"

"For an invalid?" said Nora, sourly, from the kitchen door.

"Yes. At least, a man weary to death." In the exclamations, she slipped away to the bakery, cursing herself. Carla looked up from the fireplace, and her eyes went wide. Alissandra forced her breath in and out.

"We should have made more white bread. Fine, delicate white bread." She drew a deep breath. "We shall do so now. We have a little—that which could not be divvied out evenly. Bring it. Fit for an invalid as well as a king."

Carla gasped. "The hunters returned?"

"One. Looking like death. More may follow." She looked at the flour. "Bring him the bread, but see if Nora has broth, first. He might not even be able to eat it unless he soaks it first. He's that weary."

Carla scrambled quickly enough, and went off with the tray. Alissandra started to measure the flour.

It did not surprise her that she had mixed and kneaded the dough, calming herself, before Carla returned, bubbling over. Alissandra set her to form loaves, but she babbled all the same.

"It was the courtier who thought white bread too fancy for him! He did not look so scornful now!"

"What has he said?" said Alissandra, as patiently as she could, and put aside more loaves to rise. "About the hunt? And the other hunters?"

"Uh—" Carla looked abashed.

After a minute, Alissandra said, "Can you finish this? The first loaves are ready to go in."

Carla nodded. Alissandra wiped her floury hands on her apron and went out again.

The inn's servants, and the villagers, and some even of the travelers, clumped about tables in the taproom, but the courtier sat alone. Rosa sat by him, helping with bread and broth, and Bernardo hovered, nearby.

Alissandra glided in, lightly as she could, and asked what had happened.

"A golden stag," said Bernardo, softly. "Leapt in their path, and they all gave chase. He did not master himself until he was alone in the forest with his horse all but foundered, and the sunset all scarlet."

"He's lucky he got out." After a moment, she added, "Is anyone keeping watch?"

Bernardo nodded. "Half the village at least. And a third of the travelers, I suspect. One hopes it's not like that rat-catcher—"

A shout came from outside. The rush to the door meant she could only stand and wait, but soon men had borne in two more hunters—neither of them the king, but both noblemen.

Alissandra slipped outside as the fastest way back to the bakery, where she could look out despite the uproar—and saw that three more returned. The stables were all astir with the horses, all five looking as foundered as the first steed. One stable boy loudly asked if they were expected to save them all. Frederick whapped him one on the ear.

Alissandra turned back to the bakery and bent her attention to the bread. News flittered in as one by one courtiers reappeared, dazed, exhausted, talking of a golden stag and unable to remember when last they had seen the king.

* * *

"Midnight's coming soon," said Carla, hovering by the door.

Alissandra sighed. She had always hated the tales where a hero had to rescue some princess by enduring the torments of goblins until midnight. . . and now she wished she had not remembered that tale. Happier, perhaps, to have remembered how King Matteo's grandmother had come to the ball at midnight, in rags, and his grandfather had said then and there that she was the woman he wished to marry. . . which would not happen here. Even if he had met a woman he wished to marry on the wayside.

For a moment, she toyed with baking more bread. But they had made the brown and the white, enough for both the hunting party and the travelers. More would go to waste. They might even, pushing in and pulling out loaves from the oven, burn themselves out of weariness.

On top of that, it only diverted her somewhat, and perhaps Carla not at all, with the way she darted about for news.

"Wisest to go to bed," she told Carla, as softly as she could. Carla's face set in sullen lines. "Waiting up all night will not aid the king."

But as Carla swanned off—not, she thought, toward her bed—Alissandra sighed. Waiting all night would not aid the king, but she could not sleep.

She would walk about the inn, once, she told herself. Cooler air would help her. Then she could at least rest, even if she could not sleep.

In the taproom, fewer people were waiting. Bernardo had sent off the returned hunters to bed—if the murmurs were true, all the hunters except the king himself—and shooed all the gawkers off from the room. Every scrap of broth and bread had vanished at least. The clock had nearly reached midnight.

Commotion still reigned in the stables. She walked past them, toward fields now soaked with dew. She saw something white, moving across the fields from the forest.

For several minutes, as she walked toward it, she tried to remember any white horse among the hunters', though she felt certain there had been none. It trudged toward her, summoning up memories of tales, where lords and ladies rode white horses and meant no good to anyone they met. The rider on it looked like a dead man, bound to the saddle. She stopped.

The rider lifted his head. For a moment, she saw only a worn and haggard face, a fit match for the mount. Then she recognized the king.

Words clogged in her mouth and would not escape. She rushed to take the reins—King Matteo's hands were icy—and lead the horse forward. Then torchlight fell on her, and to her relief, someone else shouted.

Her shoulders slumped with relief, and the crowd pushed her aside as they came to take both King Matteo and his horse. Even in the orange torchlight, he looked pale as bone. She hurried back to the Princess's Rest, calling for blankets and garnering surprised looks from the maids. None of the other hunters had been cold.

Which, she guessed, meant that King Matteo had suffered more than they had.

Carla appeared with white bread while they were still slipping the king to one bench. Nora came on her heels with broth. Alissandra told them, softly, that she did not think the king could eat even that.

Lizina appeared with an armful of blankets, and King Matteo submitted to being swathed like a child. They did manage to coax some broth, though no bread, into him.

"Bed," announced Bernardo. "Sleep is his only chance. And the rest of you fools need your sleep as well!"

Lizina said, softly, "I will stay up to see to it that he does not take a turn for the worse in the night."

From their faces, few intended to contest the honor. One said something about a sick prince and how whoever had stayed the night with him had vanished, but Lizina showed no signs of fear.

Alissandra headed up the stairs, and found herself yawning and unsteady. Tales of King Leandro flooded back to her, and other kings and queens, princes and princesses, whom evil will had injured and bewitched, so that a magical cure was discovered. It would not take long for fools to start looking for an ogre's feathers, or a talking fox.

She had seen no injuries, not so much as a bloodstain, but that meant little.

* * *

She woke slowly, feeling dazed. It took her more than a minute to see Lizina's empty bed, and remember why.

It took her several more before she made it down the stairs. She peeked into the taproom. The travelers ate and headed out with almost as much haste as usual. The noble hunters ate, and looked far less weary, but no more happy, than last night.

There was no sign of the king.

Back in the kitchen, Lizina sat with a bowl of porridge, looking far too serene for a woman who sat up all night at a sick bed.

"No better," said Lizina. "He did not change all night. The grooms were talking about a horse litter."

"So they are," piped up a stable boy. "All talk."

"He said nothing during the night," added Lizina, in perfect calm, as if she were already familiar with the question.

With a cold weight in her stomach, Alissandra went to dish up her own porridge. She did not dare sit next to Lizina with all the questioners approaching her.

Carla slipped in beside her and whispered she had started the brown bread this morning.

"We shall have to watch whether more or less is needed," whispered back Alissandra.

"Travelers have to eat," said Carla. "Always."

Alissandra looked at her bowl. So they did, and so did all the people of the village and the inn. Even if the king lay dying. She grimaced and ate and did not speak of his death. For one thing, she doubted anyone in the building did not think of it.

Though, when she finished, a new question occurred to her. "Was that really the king's horse?" She garnered glances, and added, "I know it wasn't white when he rode it out."

"It is," said a groom. "We never saw any such thing, but it's the king's blood bay horse all right."

Alissandra winced.

When they started to set up the litter, she went out to gawk like many another. Grooms cursed the stable boys, copiously, and one even lay in the litter to make sure it would bear the king's weight.

"While the horses stand," grumbled old Martin. "It'll be another matter when they jounce him down the road." She glanced sideways at him, but he did not assert his authority.

One groom led out the king's horse. Alissandra flinched. Broad daylight made it look even more ghostly than it had the night before. Its head hung as it plodded along. She wondered that they thought to bring it, even with the slow pace they would have to set.

"Who is the king's heir?" said some traveler.

Every gaze turned on him.

"Surely the heir to the throne should aid the king in his distress," said the man quickly, and people turned, reluctantly, away.

Chapter 9

News did not come.

Travelers came, of course. The king's unending illness could not stop merchants. Other travelers declared themselves in search of golden apples or the water of life or a golden blackbird, which would heal the king. Still others, going the other way, proclaimed themselves masters of the healing arts who would have him out of his sickbed before the next day was out. Though, Alissandra noted, those ones were never heard of again after their stay at the Rest, and taking the road toward the castle.

Still, they came, noting that if the king had not promised a reward for the one who healed him, still it would be only just and right.

"After all," said one freckled lass, her eyes bright with hope and ambition over her ale, "the land needs a king. There were—white ladies walking the lands about my village, all ball gowns and fans, walking in the mud, leaving no footprints. It can't have meant anything good. The ladies never do. We need the king."

Alissandra gave her her bread and cheese. "We will rejoice in any success of yours."

The lass raised her cup of ale. "I'll be sure to agree if you ever claim to have known Queen Rosetta before she cured the king."

Alissandra managed to keep her smile fixed. If Rosetta managed to cure the king, it would be better than before, even with a bumptious queen.

But when the travelers had headed off to bed, she wandered out to the stables and, in the gloom of straw and horses, asked the grooms and stable boys if there were tales of lords and ladies.

Little Niko looked up from currying a horse. "Tales? Of course there are tales, there are always tales—they blame lords and ladies for tangles in their horse's tails."

"When they should blame you!" roared Martin, throwing a curry comb at Niko's head. Niko ducked. Martin looked at her. "Of course there are tales. Woodsmen who claim to have seen the golden stag in the forest. Pack of them are all liars!" He snorted. "Half say they've killed it, and they'll cure the king with its heart."

"And," said Alissandra, "none at all of ladies ready for a ball? Walking about the roads?"

One groom laughed, a short bark, as he looked up from a horse hoof. "That was just old Zanni. Wandering about drunk. Bernardo should have cut his ale off sooner."

"But—" One stable boy looked about. "The merchant said it, too. Saw them near the castle when they left, that was this morning."

Silence fell, but for the horses who went on eating and stamping in their stalls without any heed for the tales.

"Heard the news of King Oswald?" said Odo, the biggest and burliest of the grooms, his heartiness sounding forced. "Died in his bed, he did, of old age, with seven strong sons all hale and hearty, and seven kingdoms to split up among them."

"That won't make the merchants happy," said Martin. "Once they each have their king, the next thing you know, they have forests on their borders, to get through."

"With dragons and witches and unicorns," said Odo.

"And golden stags," said a stable boy deep in the gloom.

Silence fell again. Alissandra sighed. King Matteo did not even have a brother king, so that a nephew could be his heir.

* * *

"You don't seem ready for bed," said Lizina, dryly.

"I'm not." Alissandra glanced over. Their lone candle cast odd patterns of pale light and shadow on the raw wood of the slanted roof; it struck Lizina's cheek but left her face mostly dark and unreadable.

"With all these tales of ladies walking about at night—I can't sleep. I want to *see*!" She let her breath out. "I saw the first hunter, I saw the king—this, too, might be part of that. And I can't sleep!"

Lizina's mouth pursed. Alissandra did not quite dare leave in the silence.

"Beautiful young maidens," said Lizina, "should not walk alone of a night. Especially when there are ladies who might *take* you."

Alissandra marshaled her arguments.

"I can be dressed in a minute."

* * *

No one noticed them as they inched out of the inn. Most of the good villagers and travelers had gone to bed—and the bad ones, as well. Even by moonlight, only a cat darting across a beaten path could be seen. A gray cat across a gray path into the gray flowers and grass spreading in the ditch. And nothing more as they walked past the village, and the fields, toward the trees.

Alissandra let out her breath as they climbed up a slope, nearing its height; the road crossed another nearby, and a narrow path wound up to the top of the hill itself.

"When I was a child, my nursemaid told me that owls' reputed wisdom was not really well thought of among the birds. Most of it consisted of knowing disreputable things that good little birds, and princesses, who went to bed at a proper hour, managed to avoid."

Lizina smiled a little. Then Alissandra blinked. Lizina was not a pale gray and white, colorless by moonlight. As if noticing her expression, Lizina blinked. Alissandra glanced aside. She could make out the colors of the ditch's growth, green with flowers of blue and gold. And past that—

It glowed against the night, rising between two hills. The king's castle might show as colorful as the dawn in the sunlight, but this castle glowed like a brighter moonlight, and cast the shadows to prove it.

"Lords and ladies," said Alissandra, her mouth dry, feeling half a fool. Who else could build a castle so?

No—two castles—or three—other lights glowed from farther away, one fiery red, one golden. The turrets were just barely visible over the hilltops, but their form was clear enough for her to be certain. She thought there was a third, a silver one—not quite as pure white as what lay before her—but a hillside stood in the way. She forced her breath out. And when she had come looking for them, at that.

"They'll be down by dawn, I dare say," she said.

Lizina nodded. Then—"Quick! Out of the way!"

Alissandra blinked and obeyed, glad they were in the crossroads, and she could jump to the road—though she sprawled on the dirt. Heavy hoofbeats drummed. She had only time to see great black horses dragging a heavy black carriage, with no coachman, before it charged by them at such a pace that they would have been trampled, or thrust in the ditch.

For a moment, Alissandra caught a glimpse through the window. She stared after the carriage, trying to tell herself that in so brief a glimpse of a pale and sickly face, she could not have been certain that King Matteo had ridden inside.

"I think—I think—" She raised her hand to point. "I think that I need to climb that hill."

Lizina's eyebrows went up.

"However narrow and steep the path—still I need to climb it." She forced a smile. "And we do not need to keep near the ditch, ready to throw ourselves in."

Lizina walked behind her. The path was so narrow that tall grass lashed their skirts with dew, but it reached the height of the hill.

The black carriage had slowed in its passage and trundled up toward a building that had not stood there an hour earlier. Aglow with silver, gold, and fiery red, the hall had great airy windows that let Alissandra glimpse a dancing floor behind.

Something odd and shadowy lay in a circle about it—far too far away for her to be sure of it.

The black carriage was not the first. A silvery carriage let down dancers in silvery ball gowns and finery—lords and ladies, one after another—more than that carriage could possibly hold. A golden carriage and a fiery one waited behind. The black carriage fell in line.

Before it reached the door, as the next two carriages discharged their ball-goers, the dancing floor swelled with tiny figures, awaiting the first dance, agleam by the lights of that hall, but when the black carriage rolled up, all the figures ceased their motions and looked only at its door.

He staggered out, alone. Alissandra bit her lip. So far away, she told herself, she could not know it was King Matteo.

He lifted his head. Even at this distance, the despair in every line was clear.

Two ladies, in silver, came forward to take him by the arm, and Alissandra felt a hand on her arm, tugging her back.

Lizina whispered. "I think—I think it might be wise to not listen too closely to the music."

Alissandra's mouth pursed, but she let Lizina draw her back. They walked down to the inn in silence. Then they went up to their beds. There being, Alissandra thought as she lay down, nothing else to do.

She lay abed, wondering. Among other things, whether she would have slept better, bothered by the ignorance.

* * *

The castles, and the hall, were gone by morning. Still, rumors were sibilant about the village. No one else mentioned seeing King Matteo, but tales were wild, of castles and carriages—some bold souls claimed to have seen them drawn by dragons or gryphons—of the dancing hall, even, though fewer of those.

They came again, night after night. The rumors all but swamped the tales of how the king sickened. Even as the days wound on, and Alissandra heard the carriage thunder by at night, and tales of the castles by day.

After a week, she sought out Lizina where she folded sheets as white as swans. "All the bold souls must have gone on quests. No one has ventured to rescue the king."

Lizina dropped a folded sheet on the pile. "Including you."

Alissandra opened her mouth and shut it again. Some minutes, and several sheets, later, she said, "I am not bold. I fear that circle about the dancing hall."

Lizina was half hidden by the sheet she held up. "Their carriages travel through it safely enough." She folded the sheet in half.

"I am not bold enough to try to steal one," said Alissandra dryly. "And I do not think they would stop to take me up, even if I dressed grandly enough for the ball." She looked down at her floury skirt and hands. "And you saw what I packed."

"Even if you had packed your finery," said Lizina, "they might regard it as shoddy."

"As shoddy as Tattercoats," said Alissandra. "And they don't need directions from me."

Lizina smiled. "But—if you went to one of their castles, you might learn something of use."

* * *

Lizina, ghost-like, appeared in the doorway as Carla hurried off to bed, and Alissandra laid everything else to be ready in the morning.

"Still not wise for a maiden to wander alone?" she said, and Lizina smiled.

"When was it ever wise?"

Minutes later, swathed in gray cloaks, they stole along a path. At least with the castles appearing always in the same places, they did not have to await the darkness. The sky had just barely turned shades of delicate pink and yellow in the west.

It had turned fiery shades of scarlet, crimson, and flame, and darkened overhead, and the first dew had formed on the grass, before the castle appeared ahead of them. For a moment, blinking, Alissandra wondered whether it had risen up, or just appeared, but they had no time to linger while she wondered.

They hurried up the hill. In the valley below, the castle stood, and silvery bright lords and ladies emerged from doorways in pale shifts and shirts.

Not, Alissandra noted, ball gowns. Not even finery. Her teeth fastened on her lower lip, and slowly, with care, she edged just far enough down the hillside that she would not be silhouetted against the sky.

One lady, her silver blond hair all but floating about her, started to twirl. Around her, circling about, glinting in the castle's light, came dew drops. They converged on her, and she stood in a gown of gleaming gray.

"Dew!" Another damsel tossed her head, her hair flying. Her light voice carried far. "How fortunate for you that it fell so soon."

"And you will try something harder?" The dew-clad lady glanced over her shoulder.

The other one smiled, and began to twirl. Slowly, silvery pale light arched in. In—Alissandra scowled—two spirals. She could see them arching away and up. Their path rose higher and higher, and Alissandra could just barely trace them to the two evening stars.

She looked away, sharply, and stared at the innocent wildflowers bedecking the ditch.

"They conjure starlight to amuse themselves!" she whispered to Lizina. "How can I—how can anyone—free someone from such power?"

"Everything on earth has its weaknesses," said Lizina.

Alissandra looked back. More lords and ladies filled the grassy sward, and they no longer studied the one conjuring clothes. In small groups, at most, some watched while others twirled about and then stood ready for the ball in the palest shades. Then those watchers twirled in their turn. Sooner than seemed possible, the field held only people in radiant array, who would overawe any ball Alissandra had ever attended, making every ball-goer she had ever seen before look as dowdy as an autumnal wildflower, gone to seed.

Then the carriage arrived. Laughing and chortling, they streamed within, paying no heed to how they could fit. The last pulled the door shut behind them, and the carriage moved off, gleaming. She watched it until the shadows of the trees hid it from her.

Alissandra forced her breath out.

"Come," said Lizina. Looking thoughtful, she turned back toward the inn.

Alissandra rolled her eyes. She did have to return, but what urgency was there? Rushing would only give them less time to think.

The village had come into shadowy sight again before Lizina spoke.

"They conjure things," she said, slowly, as if her thoughts were still forming. "Everything, it seems."

Alissandra's eyebrows went up. Like the flowers that could fall from her hair and hands—"Don't they always?"

"Such lords and ladies often crave things that are real and unconjured. Especially marvels."

"You sound," said Alissandra dryly, "like you have a plan."

Lizina shrugged. "One to propose, but I do not have a marvel. Such as a silver feather."

Alissandra stopped in her tracks.

"The feather," observed Lizina idly, "did come to you."

Chapter 10

Alissandra glanced about the bakery. "All set?"

Her eyes huge, Carla nodded. She did not look ready to protest her good fortune of being able to show she could manage the bakery all by herself. Yet. Alissandra remembered her first days alone, and wondered whether that would continue in the morning.

All the more reason to use Carla's willingness now. She pulled up her hood. The silver feather already lay in her belt pouch, and she stole away over the grass, taking not to touch the pouch.

Lizina was likewise swathed in a cloak. Her cheek and jaw were illuminated in the flowery sunset light, but then she turned her face away, and the two of them scurried up the path like two little ghosts. They garnered glances, having set out early enough that some souls still were aboard, but they walked on too quickly for anyone to question them.

Across the fields—through the pastures—up the hill—her heart started to hammer—and down the other side. Where, on the grassy swards very edge, she started to shed her outer garments, one by one. Lizina gathered and folded them neatly.

Alissandra, standing in only her shift, took out the silvery feather. It glowed in the gloom. Lizina put the clothes away in her bag and hurried away.

As Alissandra had urged her to do when they made the plan. She had even said that she should leave them at the hilltop, so that Lizina did not have to come down and go back up; it was Lizina who gently said it was not far.

She felt cold.

She turned her attention to the feather before she could succumb to the desire to run after Lizina and never return. The feather gleamed, abruptly, brighter, and her own shadow was stark on the grass. She let out her breath. The castle had arrived.

Alissandra drew her breath in and out, reminded herself that she had to look back at the feather as if it were lovelier, and looked up.

The silvery castle shone. All about lords and ladies streamed from doorways. And—Alissandra cocked an eyebrow and looked back at the feather. It did indeed look lovelier. She took it by the quill and held it up to admire—and to display, with a scrap of subtlety.

Her heart pattered more quickly. She had come to barter, not to keep.

As soft-footed as cats, the lord and ladies padded up to her, and circled about. Their gazes avid, they did not even begin their conjurations.

"What causes you to tarry, you fools? Do you think the night will linger so you can dance as long as ever if you arrive hours late?" The lady's voice rang over the sward, and the circle about her parted, as if to form a path.

At the end of this pathway, a lady stood, already gowned in silver, more radiant and regal than the gowns Alissandra remembered from the night before. The lords and ladies bowed and curtseyed.

She is not your queen, Alissandra told herself firmly. It was easier to bring back the memories of her days in court and stand straight than she would have dreamed.

"My dear little child," said the lady, her voice sweet, "What in the world does such a marvel do in your clumsy little hands?"

Alissandra shrugged, and shifted her hand. Light glinted. For a moment, all was silence.

"What would you take, in return for that father?" said the lady, with care.

Alissandra drew in her breath. "Neither for silver nor for gold, neither for wish nor for charm." She shifted her hand again, and heard longing gasps all about. "Only for music and dancing. Give me a gown that I may safely wear, bear me safely to the ball, let me dance safely there, and let me return in safety and go unhindered and unharmed henceforth."

Silence was long.

"You drive a hard bargain, my lass!"

Alissandra shrugged. Then she shifted her hand. "Then, I could always keep my silver father for myself. That would be consolation."

Moment inched by. Were they haggling in the market, no doubt another offer would counter hers. But this lady had spoken of haste. . . .

"I myself will attire you in dove gray," said the lady.

"Do you accept my bargain?" said Alissandra. "In full? With a whole heart?"

The lady nodded. Alissandra did not move.

"I agree. . . ."

Moments later, she added, "In full. With a whole heart."

Her hand went up. Gray started to form about Alissandra.

With shrieks of alarm—look at the time!—lords and ladies threw themselves into their enchantments until the swirling lights made Alissandra dizzy. She closed her eyes for a moment as wispy cloth settled on her, and opened them to see a shining gown as lovely as any about her. And a fan on her belt, with silvery feathers that had to be false.

Their consternation over the time had made them seem almost human. This sobered her. Though it did remind her that the promise was binding. That at least was true of lords and ladies.

The silvery carriage stood with its door open. Alissandra drew a deep breath and joined the stream of dancers going in before anyone could urge her to come along—or suggest that she did not have to demand they fulfill the bargain. Stepping inside, for a moment, felt as unsettling as walking onto a barge while the river made it bob. But, though she could not quite tell how, the interior had seats for all. Alissandra sat beneath silver flower etched into the leather wall, and the ladies about her began to babble about how many dances they would dance, and which ones—

Alissandra's mouth twitched. She folded her hands in her lap. At least she knew the dances by name, and all their steps as well. But after a minute, she noticed they never spoke of who would partner them.

The ride, strangely enough, took exactly as long as she would expect for a carriage to move between the castle and the dancing hall. Remembering tales from her governess, she gathered her skirts and stepped down with care in the midst of the crowd, neither stumbling on the step nor leaping over it. She glanced back at the press of dancers, and caught a glimpse of a golden-haired woman, the only one looking back.

At least, she told herself, she could not be picked out in the crowd. She proceeded in with the crowd. Musicians clad in discreet gray and brown stood in the corner—tiny brown figures, many dwarfed by their instruments. Candles glowed in massive array, some with flaxen flames, but others in silver, and still others as fiery red as a hearth fire. Already the room was warmer than the evening air.

The crowd spread out over the dance floor. Alissandra stepped swiftly with them. Already the gold-clad lords and ladies flooded in. She picked her way to one side, where the flood could not bear her back, where she could see out the door, where the golden carriage stood. She took up her fan and hoped, as she fanned herself and hid her face, that she would not be conspicuous as she waited.

"Already overwrought, my lady?" A tall, elegant lord appeared by her, gleaming like the moon.

Alissandra forced out a little laugh. "I could not have dreamed of such a ball."

He laughed—a light sound, not reassuring. "Since you asked to dance safely, I am to be the first of your partners. You will dance every dance you wish to dance, and not one more." He held out his arm. She could see the fiery-clad dancers arriving behind him.

"Surely you do not begin the measures before all the dancers have arrived?"

He hesitated. "It is best to take a place in the figures, to be ready for the dance."

She nodded. "Very well." To buy time, she folded her fan and opened it again. "But I—I confess that I am such a country chit that I wish to see all their finery as they arrive." She forced a smile. "In this finery, I can even watch them here, and not gawk from the roadside, surrounded by geese!"

"Ah, but here comes the last." He nodded toward the doorway. There stood King Matteo. Dressed in black, pale as a bone, his face already worn and exhausted, he looked about the ball room. She did not know whether he actually saw any of them. Certainly, he showed no sign of recognizing her, though, between the finery and his having seen her no more than half a dozen times, he would not.

"Come, let us find our places!"

Alissandra let him draw her among the dancers, silver, golden, and fiery red, but could not help glancing back. When her partner scowled, she forced a giggle.

"He does look striking, doesn't he? So *stark* among all this glitter."

She realized then that she must have spoken into a lull, for scores of lords and ladies looked at her. She laughed again, lightly.

"Who would be the easiest to find at this ball? Certainly him. You could pick him out at a glance."

She turned to her self-appointed partner. He stood as still as a stone. "Then, I was promised dancing, not looking about a dance floor." She looked, pointedly, at his arm. He did not argue—not even that it was her fault, since she was the one who had dallied before the dancing—only bowed and offered his arm.

The first dance was frantic of step, and she was as flushed as every other dancer by the end. The second was scarcely slower, and for the third, she pled exhaustion to her third partner. There were, to be sure, lords and ladies seated by the side of the dancing floor.

"Though I would be honored if you would sit this one out with me."

He smiled and bowed and offered to fetch her refreshments.

"Oh no," she said, fanning herself. "I wish only to rest. Not to eat or drink."

Nor would she, even when her mouth burned with dryness, and her stomach growled with hunger, as they would no doubt do before the dawn. She had not even thought to ask to eat and drink safely; she knew too well what their food and drink could do. . . .

Which drew her back to the king. He, of course, did not sit out the dance, or any other. She watched with care, trying to angle toward him even as she sat out every third dance. They gave him neither food nor drink, but he danced every dance. As none of the lords or ladies did.

And when she had won her way to figure next to his, he, in mid-dance, collapsed on the floor and did not stir.

Commotion encircled him. Lords dragged him to his feet, and ladies fanned him until he opened his eyes again. Then they shoved him into the arms of another partner.

Alissandra felt as if her gown were made of snow, and it was no surprise that it did not melt, because she was as cold as it was. She accepted a new partner's proffered hand, and let him draw her back into the measure. It was three dances before she had the wits to attend to anything except the steps.

Then she set her mouth and angled toward the king again, watching how each partner came to his hand as the dance ended. Then where each lady had stood in the figures before. Then—her eyes narrowed—she brought her partner to that place.

Easily, as if it were one of the steps, she turned to the king and took his hand. Perhaps one or two dancers started. No one objected, or moved toward her.

Then—she looked at King Matteo's haggard face, and knew they had nothing to fear. He could not recognize her as the baker at the Princess's Rest, or even as a mortal woman. His hand felt cold even on hers.

She yielded him to his next partner, not caring that the figures would not bring them together again. She sat out the next dance, and every other one after, and tried not to look at the king. He staggered through every dance. When she danced, she wondered that she managed to not fumble the steps.

Until, finally, the carriages pulled up again, and the dancers began to regret the dawn but stream toward the doors. King Matteo, first of all, was handed into his carriage. Then they poured into their own. Alissandra managed to put herself in the flood of silvery dancers, and collapse within the silvery carriage. Smooth though the journey was, she managed to keep awake until they tumbled out again. The sky had started to turn gray, and dissolve the stars.

The lady, smiling like a pleased cat, stalked toward Alissandra. Alissandra suppressed her yawn and produced the silver feather. The lady snatched it from her fingers, the dancers flitted away like startled birds, and the air was filled with their sweet, mocking laughter. Both the castle and the dancers dissolved more swiftly than the morning mist.

Also, noted Alissandra, her gown. She was left standing in her shift, barefoot, in the morning gray, far colder than the evening. Lizina hurried over the dew-laden grass with her clothes. She rushed to pull them on. Then, weary as she was, walked quickly along the path to warm herself.

Lizina asked no questions on the way.

* * *

Carla looked askance at her dew-laden skirt but said nothing as Alissandra inspected the bakery.

Or when Lizina came in. She went on kneading the dough.

"Can you trust her?" said Lizina. "Do you know her well?"

"I can keep a secret," said Carla, turning, her arms and face marred with flour.

"Ah, but will you?" said Lizina, and Alissandra frowned, wondering why Lizina did not just talk with her somewhere else.

"Oh, yes," said Carla, eagerly. Lizina's smile broadened a little, and more hesitantly, "Oh, yes."

Alissandra let her breath out. She did not know, herself, who Lizina was—but then, she still did not know who Donata was.

"I kept my own secret," said Carla, soft-voiced. "I ran away from home. After my mother died, my father said that we three girls had to keep house, but my oldest sister mended a shirt, and my middle sister washed a dish, and they said they had done their share, and made me do all the rest. And ran out to catch our father and complain that I wasn't doing mine, and would lie about it. And they kept it up.

"But one day, my father asked them what they wanted from the fair—not me, since I wasn't doing my share. So one asked for a gown like all the clouds in the sky, and the other for a gown like all the flowers in a field. But they went gadding about, so I didn't do my work. One day off didn't seem like too much to take. And I got dressed up in our mother's wedding gown, like sun and starlight.

"When my father came home, he said he was astounded at so lovely a lady, and that he was a widower, and that he wanted to know who I was."

Alissandra scowled.

"So I stuck my nose in the air and told him that I would not listen to cozening. If he gave me the two gowns he had brought as proof of his good faith, I would tell him who I was. So he did, and I did, and he threw me out of the house."

She giggled. "I took the gowns. And the work's easier here than at home. And their house must be all but a ruin now."

"You'll have to keep this secret longer than your own, likely enough," said Alissandra.

Carla nodded solemnly.

"I went to see these lords and ladies and what they do of a night."

Carla blinked. The dough dripped from her fingers, unheeded.

"It hardly did any good. I saw King Matteo up close, I can confirm they have enchanted him, I even danced with him—"

Lizina's eyebrows went up.

"One dance, no more. He switches partners for every dance. Not only to be *courteous*, but none of them dance all night. It would exhaust them as badly as he is exhausted. They would ail as badly as he does." She drew a deep breath and forced herself to speak in a measured manner. "At that, it would not have mattered if I had danced every one with him. He did not know me. I doubt he would know anyone, even those he is accustomed to seeing in finery. He did not speak, either. If he knows how the enchantment works, still I would not learn it from him."

Carla gawked.

Lizina shifted her weight. "Do the lords and ladies gossip where you can hear?"

"Not on any matter that could help me." She hesitated. "Though I did not try to listen." So bent on dancing with the king. . . .

Lizina's mouth pursed. "I wonder if anyone else can help him. There have been no tales from the castle about how the king is carried off each night in a carriage, and returns more weary in the morning. The lords and ladies probably enchant them as well."

Carla's eyes seemed ready to bulge from her head. Alissandra glanced at her hands.

"That's enough kneading," she said, with sudden sharpness.

Carla flinched and blushed, and started to shape the dough into loaves, to rise.

"I could have danced all night, if I accepted enough partners." Alissandra described it all in detail, Lizina listening gravely, Carla with a rapt attention that she tried to conceal, though it was hard when the loaves were all set aside to rise, and she did not budge.

"There were—" Alissandra hesitated. "There were back rooms that I never went in. They were lit less brightly than the ballroom—"

And the only way to discover what lay there would be to return.

* * *

It had grown colder this night, and they had walked farther. She would not have managed if Carla had not urged her off to bed, with promises to manage all the bakery.

Lizina neatly folded her clothes up and put them away before she withdrew, leaving Alissandra holding the golden feather, glowing in the golden sunset light. She shivered and waited. The sunset darkened, through blood red, to a crimson shade. The golden castle blossomed before her, more radiant than the dawn.

Alissandra drew a deep breath and bent her head, to look enraptured with the feather.

"So! She comes!"

A mass of lords and ladies filled the sward she stood on. A regal, towering lady, ablaze with sunset gold, plowed through them, and they pulled aside, bowing and curtseying, before turning their attention back to Alissandra.

"Having offered our dear friend such a feather last night, only now does she come with one for me!"

Alissandra looked slowly up. "Why, my lady, what would be the point of bringing it last night? I would not deem you more petty and mean-spirited than she was. I would think you willing to give as great a boon in return as she did—all the more in that I will sell it for neither silver nor gold, neither wish nor charm."

The lady looked indulgent. "So, you wish to go to the ball that much?"

Alissandra shrugged. "I could always stay, and keep my golden feather."

Moments later, dressed in sunset glow that had faded from the sky, Alissandra watched as the lords and ladies clad themselves in ripe wheat, or sunrise, or candlelight.

You turn into an old hand in dealing with ladies, she told herself.

* * *

"O," said Alissandra, "I could not dance another step!"

The golden-clad lord bowed, and started to open his mouth.

"But," she said, swiftly, and smiled, "I would love to watch, if you joined the measures. Surely I have never seen such dancing in all my days. A marvel and a wonder."

He did not move for a moment, his face as emotionless as a mask. She kept her smile as mask-like. She did not even glance at the chairs, so that he could suggest sitting out with her, or tables, so that he could offer food. He bowed and swept off in the resplendent crowd, with its single dark figure.

King Matteo had not collapsed this night. Yet.

She let her breath out and drew back. To not interfere with the measures, she told herself; that was what it would look like. No one would notice that she eased toward one of the shadowed, arched door-ways.

She drew no comment, even when she reached and stood in one. A glimpse within showed no lords playing cards, no ladies exchanging spite-edged gossip, nothing to eavesdrop on. Still, the air felt cooler there, without the blazing arrays of candles, and the frenzied dancers. She eased back into it. She could always claim that it refreshed her.

The room lay the length of the ball room, for all the dozens of door-ways. Bands of light lay across the shadows, like gussets set in a gown. She picked her way down it. The lady had not stinted on her golden slippers; she made no more sound than a butterfly alighting on flowers. At the end of the darkened room, a window stood. Within the dancing floor, they were none—they would only be mirrors between the light inside and the darkness without—but here, she drew close enough to peer out.

Things wriggled on the ground. She started, leaping back, her heart pounding, before she knew them for snakes. Like the ones that had menaced the birds. One fixed her with a gaze so baleful that she drew back, and fled the length of the back room before she stopped to bring her harsh breathing and frantic heart under mastery again.

There was a window there, too. She did not look out.

But the hours would pass all too soon. She braced herself and came out. A bevy of ladies, growing matronly, laughed.

"Come to dance again?" said one, attired in spider's web silver. She almost managed to sound maternal.

"I was anxious," said Alissandra. "Such an open place this is. Why, anyone could intrude!" She widened her eyes. "And even bear off the king!"

They laughed again, more amused. "Hardly!" said the one in spider's web.

Another, her gown as fiery orange as a bonfire, smiled in satisfaction. "We have a guard that does not want to guard us. Loathsome, poisonous snakes and toads."

"Such as fall from the lips of princesses who speak rudely to great ladies," said a third, as golden as sunrise, and fanned herself. "Or did. Nowadays we find their number quite sufficient for our purposes, and have varied our curses."

"Quite enough, indeed," said the spider-web one. "They are drawn with poisonous hatred to all that is bright and beautiful. As long as our enchantments keep them from encroaching farther, they will form a guard, and bit with fury all who try to pass, since they—" She smiled. "—can not bite us."

"But," said Alissandra, "we came by carriage."

The sunrise one tossed her hand in the air. "The roads as well."

"While the carriage come and leave, only," said the bonfire one. "So we—and you—are safe between. No one will come down those roads while we dance."

"But the carriages can get through safely?"

"Oh yes," said the spider-web one.

"But the king's castle is so far away—" She looked among them, from face to face. "Only the strongest enchantments could do such a thing."

They all laughed, merrily.

"His carriage has special horses, to ensure it," said the sunrise one. "Nightmares, they sometimes call them." She lowered her voice. "They do not have eyes. They can *smell* out the road. Neither fog nor storm nor magically laid gloom can keep him from our revels!

The bonfire one nodded. "Only if someone hauled him out on the way and held him through any enchantment could they seize him, and they could not even stop the carriage!"

"How *thorough*!" Alissandra smiled, and calculated. She should dance every—fourth—dance. To make her look delighted, but to not exhaust her too much.

* * *

She left the hall that night not in the middle of the throng, but to the edge, near enough that she could spy the black carriage.

And the horses—something about them made it hard to look—her gaze kept slipping away for no reason, leaving no impression but nausea, but she forced her gaze back, and saw a head—a horse head with no eyes.

When her gaze shifted away again, she did not try for a better look, only meekly ascended into the carriage.

* * *

The colors in the feather shifted, from red to orange, almost to yellow, and then back again to red as brilliant as a burning log.

"All I ask," said Alissandra, "is a gown that I may safely wear, being borne safely to the ball, being let to dance safely there, and leave safely, to go unharmed and unhindered."

Her voice did not sound hoarse in her own ears, and the grand lady, dressed in fire, did not seem to notice. Her heart hammered. If only she had not heard what bargain Alissandra had offered before. Or if only she would assume that Alissandra was a slovenly fool, not to ensure it again.

*　*　*

In the gleaming hall, she danced every fourth dance. Sometimes every fifth. Her heart pattered almost all the time, as she veered between fear that too few dances would alert them, hope that it would not matter whether they knew, and certainty that they were too smug to notice, however many reasons she gave them to guess.

Her fiery skirts spread about her, she watched the king dance. He ailed still more than on the last two nights, needing to be hauled to his feet three and four times. She did not even try to join his figure this night.

Then lords and ladies, sighing about the dawn, started to leave. Her heart hammering so loudly that she wondered that they did not hear it as she meekly joined the crowd. Outside, the waning crescent moon had just risen, and she bit her lip. If the lady realized what she intended, and resolved to stop her, or even whimsically decided to allow her to ride back in the carriage, all was lost—and she had used up all three of the feathers—

The lady flamed up before her. "Not you." Her dulcet voice was light, amused.

Alissandra pulled back, hoping she looked properly horrified. "But I—but I—they brought me back before—" Which at least sputtered and sounded desperate.

Laughter resounded: high, light, cruel.

"With them you bargained to be taken away again. Not with me, not with me—" The lady's smile deepened. "The feather."

Alissandra raised her head. "Unharmed and unhindered. On the other side of the snakes, I will give it." She strode off.

Out of the dancing floor, the stray light gave her a better view. Loathsome indeed. Coiling all along the way. . . .

A fiery path pushed them back, and she walked in the gap, out onto the road.

The lady appeared before her, holding out her hand. Alissandra surrendered the feather.

"The deal is done," said the lady. "And your claim to your finery is gone as well." She swept the air with a hand. The skirts and bodice dissolved, leaving her standing barefoot in her shift.

Alissandra drew a deep breath. A dancing slipper was scarcely better than no shoe at all on the road. She would have been barefoot as soon as she wore the slipper away.

Rocks, said a macabre thought, and Alissandra fled down the road before she could lose her courage. Laughter followed. She ran and ran, and when the laughter gave way to the sounds of departing coaches, she did not stop. Not until she was in silence. . . .

At least none of them had noticed what road she had fled on. Or guessed what it meant. Her breath came raggedly, and her heart throbbed in her chest, and she had no time to wait. She fished at the neck of her shift, and pulled out her comb. Then she heard the babble of water. She edged forward a little. About a curve, moonlight made the water glitter where it flowed over the road in a little ford, and Alissandra felt almost giddy. She dropped to her knees and began to wash her hands in the bitterly cold waters. Lilies flowed sweetly from her fingers, clogging the way and beyond. Her fingers grew numb, but the air was filled with sweetness.

Before she could no longer feel her hands, she stood. The heat from her running was fading, her skirts was muddy and dripping from where she had knelt on the sodden bank, but she still had the comb. Tilting her head to one side, she began to comb her hair. Roses added their scent to the air, and she walked along the roadside, hemming the way in, and crossing the road to do it again on the other side. Among ordinary horses, the youngest of foals would have no difficulty crossing this barrier, but nothing could be smelled past the sweetness.

Hooves began to clop nearer. She tucked the comb away and stood aside. Not too far—she did not want to be trampled, but she would have little time.

She drew a deep breath. Her feet were sore. Her hands were still all but numb, for all the work she had put into combing. And she was not yet done.

The hooves clopped, at a great pace, and the creaking of wheels followed. The coach hove into view, the horses thundering along, with neither reins nor coachmen.

She still could not directly look at them, but the coach, she could. And she did not mind the horses.

The horses did not even pause before they reached the flowers. Then, with a fierce, indignant whinny, they reared up, their hooves lashing at the air, their nostrils flaring. The carriage jounced behind them, and Alissandra cringed. If that hit her, either horse or carriage—

They settled a little, sniffing at the air. Close enough to safety, thought Alissandra, and though the carriage did not stay in place, she jumped up on the step and seized the door. It leapt under her hand. She grabbed with both hands, but the door did not open. She set her mouth, freed one hand to seize the window, and pulled.

King Matteo, his eyes closed, sprawled on the seat. She freed a hand again to tug on his shoulder. He stirred only enough to moan. She scrambled inside to put her arms about him and heave.

The carriage jumped again, throwing them toward the open door. She threw herself with it, trying to restrain their fall, caught her hand on the carriage and bruised it, but managed to drag King Matteo out.

He groaned when they hit the ground, but did not rouse. She put her arms about him and heaved him farther way, winning inch after inch, and felt a burning desire to have been a nice sturdy milk maid. Her arms ached with the effort.

She staggered into the woods, brought King Matteo to lie under a maple, and concluded that was far enough. For all the ruckus, moonlight had barely filtered through the trees; little time had passed.

King Matteo did not stir. She sat under the tree and put her arms about him. He slept on, though the horses continued to rear and cry out, and the carriage was battered to bits. She shifted every now and again, trying to avoid stiffness, and the cool air started to chill her, even as the sky lightened.

She sniffed. Cool, yes, and starting to smell more of morning, and less of roses and lilies. One horse lifted its head and screamed. Her arms tightened, and the king opened his eyes. For a moment, his gaze was as hollow and unreasoning as it had been in the hall, but it sharpened as he took her in and glanced over the carriage.

Moments later, faster than their castles had sprung up, fierce and terrible, the ladies who had taken her bargains and her feathers stood about it. Their gowns were as brilliant as at the ball, but their faces were white as salt. They looked about, and their gazes settled on Alissandra. Horses and carriage alike vanished as if they had never existed, leaving not even a trace like smoke, and the ladies did not so much as twitch in their intent gazes.

The silver one said, "What is the meaning of this?"

"After you have been a guest at our balls," said the golden one.

"A strange exchange for our hospitality."

Alissandra shrugged, as best she could with King Matteo in her arms. "I gave you the feathers in return. You seemed to think them quite sufficient. You asked for nothing more, and you should not disgrace yourself by going back on what you said."

"You!"

She could not have told which one spoke with such fierce anger, but her stiff arms tightened about King Matteo.

Who stirred a little more, looking about, and then shouted, "Old mothers!"

The ladies recoiled.

"Old mothers! Old mothers!"

Then, to either side of them, there was a shift, and another one behind. Alissandra's mouth went dry. The hills moved. Or rather—her tongue touched her lips as the form came clear—three enormous figures, covered with trees and moss and ferns, but still clearly human-like in shape, roused up. They looked down on the road with eyes as yellow and round as a new risen full moon.

One spoke, in a voice deep and cavernous. "Who calls?"

"One who calls for judgment," said King Matteo. "Tell me, old mothers. These three sold me for feathers. This one bought me. To whom do I belong?"

Laughter boomed out over hills and forest. Three voices spoke as one, resounding: "Forsake the ones who sold you, for her who bought you!"

He smiled, and sank back against Alissandra, his eyes closing.

The ladies' face contorted, sharpened, looked less than human. But one old mother waved a hand at them, and they were gone, like a candle flame blown out, save that they left not even smoke.

Her breath went out. They vanished, thought Alissandra, as thoroughly as the horses and carriage had.

Then the old mothers settled back down, once again hills. Alissandra wondered what streams and stones had been shifted by their motion and watched them a long time after they went still again. Birds started to sing, in the dawn chorus that she would have expected in less enchanted lands.

The king shifted in her arms, and she turned to him. He was smiling upon her.

And then gave a startled cry, and reached toward his throat—toward, she realized, a thin, plain chain there. But under his fingers, it dissolved into nothingness.

"The spell," he said, half-dazed, "it's gone."

"Which is well," said Alissandra. "I did not have more feathers to bargain with them, for visits."

He smiled. He must have fathomed more of the gossip than had seemed possible. Then his gaze sharpened on her.

"You are Alissandra," he said. "You have been the baker at the Princess's Rest, for over the last year."

She blushed. He could not imagine she was a lady, after this, but—"I am Princess Alissandra of Elferrin. Whose sisters vanished, and whose parents promised to their rescuer the hand of one of them, and half the kingdom, and then the whole after the king dies." She drew a deep breath. "So I set out to seek my fortune. Lest anyone think I had any claim to the kingdom, and let my poor sisters languish."

Slowly he nodded. Then his mouth twitched. "How generous of you."

She flushed and looked away. A figure plodded toward them. She blinked. A figure with very pale blond hair, carrying a bundle of clothes. Matteo followed her gaze and frowned in thought.

Lizina grinned at the sight of them. "What with all the uproar, I'm surprised I found you first." She held out the bundle.

Alissandra eased free of the king, who leaned back against the tree, and glanced her over. His breath hissed out.

"You do not want to put your shoes on," he said.

She could wash the mud off in the stream, she thought, and looked down, and blinked. The blood on them was stark red, and abruptly, they hurt worse than they had before.

"You do not want to walk on them," said Matteo, half-rising before he sank again.

Lizina chuckled. "Nor do we want to carry you, Your Majesty. I spoke with peasants. Red Walt agreed to bring his cart here, though it will take some time."

Alissandra dressed, quickly, leaving her feet bare, and sat again; her feet were already glad of it.

"Then," said Matteo, "there is nothing to do now except pass the time with talk. I have seen you, o benefactor, at the Princess's Rest, but I do not know your name."

Lizina chuckled. "My name is Lizina. I came with the princess from her parents' castle."

Shortly thereafter, she sat back against another tree, as discreet as a lady-in-waiting letting her mistress talk with a wooer.

Light increased, and the warmth returned. Morning had full risen—sunrise having overtaken the gray, and then turned to blue—before the cart trundled down the road toward them. Still, Alissandra was not overly glad to see him. There had been much to talk of.

Chapter 11

Carla looked bright-eyed as she arrived with the bread. The finest white bread.

Alissandra looked up. She sat not in the main room but in that set aside for nobles—white-washed and timbered like the rest of the rooms, but with more windows, and set apart from the crowd. Her feet, propped up on a stool, smelled of herbs from the ointment beneath the bandages. King Matteo had, with help, staggered into the Princess's Rest, but she had had to be carried. Bernardo had come to do it himself. She wondered if the strangeness of it was merely that it happened at the Princess's Rest, or if she had forgotten so much of being a princess.

Lizina sat in the corner, smiling a little, and sewed. She had returned to court life without trouble.

Matteo's chair was propped up with pillows, but sleeping all day had worked wonders. He did not look tired as he spoke gravely with the still dusty councilors who had ridden hard to reach them. Her mouth twitched. She wondered how long it would take him to get through all the business of the realm for the last weeks when he had ailed too much to do anything.

"We have brought the horse litter to bear you to the castle," said one councilor.

Matteo winced, but nodded.

Carla slid the bread before her, and whispered, "It's nice to be the baker."

Alissandra glanced at Matteo and blushed. Carla had served as the baker for the last three days, and would have to at least until her feet healed.

"Sire," said one clerk, "when we send word to Elferrin, we know that they will ask us how we know that this princess is the lost Princess Alissandra. And not some servant who turned the princess into a bird and claimed her place."

Matteo looked indignant. Lizina laughed. She produced the comb that Alissandra had brought that night.

"A basin of water would help as well," she said. Carla squeaked and ran out. Alissandra took the comb—there was no point in waiting—and shook out her hair to one side before she started to comb, and the roses started to fall: red and pink and yellow, single roses, double roses, roses with dozens of petals.

Carla, coming in, stopped so suddenly that the water sloshed, but despite her damp dress, she brought it over, and Alissandra laid aside the comb to wash her hands, and let the lilies fall.

Moments later, the maids slipped flowers from the room—no doubt to feed the rumors—and Matteo gravely told the clerk that he would have to write the letter, since he could assure the king and queen that he had seen with his own eyes that it was the princess.

Bernardo came in, during a lull, and bowed.

"Your Majesty, there is neither a queen mother nor any other princess at the royal castle. It would be most improper for the Princess Alissandra to stay there before you wed. Certainly before you are betrothed."

King Matteo lifted an eyebrow.

"She can remain here. Perhaps fitting attendants for a night or two at the city, but between, she can remain here."

"Both prudent and generous of you, Master Bernardo," said Matteo. "With the time the preparations will take."

The chamberlain bowed. "They were already speaking of how to prepare for your betrothal, Your Majesty." He shifted and bowed again. "Your Highness."

Alissandra swallowed.

"Not until my bride can stand, I trust," said Matteo.

* * *

Riding a fine dapple gray mare, as befit a princess. Traveling in a company that befit a princess. Wearing a gown that was finer than she had ever worn riding before, even as a princess. Even Lizina's gown was finer than any of her old riding gowns.

Then, she had never gone riding to arrive at such a ceremony before.

The castle before them had blossomed with banners and garlands, and all along the flower-strewn way, great crowds, wearing their finest, waved flags and cheered. Small children ran about, squealing in excitement. Sunny though the day was, the brisk breeze made all the banners and flags ripple and snap.

As befitted a princess, soon to be a queen, and their queen at that, she nodded and smiled and waved. The passage through the city seemed longer than the entire rest of the journey, and her smile felt like a mask.

They rode on. Up to the castle, over the bridge, into the radiant square, with courtiers lining every inch of the wall, and servants leaning out of the windows.

King Matteo stood at the doors to the great hall, at the top of the stairs.

Her face eased. It took nothing to smile now.

No sooner had her company arrived than he began to descend to the courtyard, to greet her. Servants ran to hand her down from her steed.

* * *

Morning sunlight came through the windows, into a bare gray room, its floor littered with cloth and trimmings.

"Gold for the wedding gown," said the head seamstress with authority. Alissandra remembered a golden gown sweeping about her, as light as thistledown, from the lady's enchantments, and held her tongue. It took some effort. The sooner she wore cloth-of-gold, the sooner she would master the art of moving in that heavy burden. And her wedding gown would at least remain a gown in the morning.

"Hold your arms out," said the seamstress.

Alissandra held her arms out. With all their flaws, the ladies could attire her much more swiftly than an entire bevy of royal seamstresses. Cloth flapped about, blue and red and green, and more crowded than the banners for her betrothal.

The feast for which had lasted late, and the seamstresses had descended early. The noblewomen appointed to attend her yawned in their chairs by the door. Lizina seemed awake enough, perched on a table and watching.

"Certainly those gowns of yours— " The head seamstress shook her head.

"Are a princess's gowns," said Lizina, mildly. "It might cause offense to imply that they are not fit for her new kingdom."

For a moment, there was stillness. Then a young seamstress said she had brought the cloth-of-gold.

"Fit or not fit," said the head seamstress, "they are not enough."

* * *

In the hallway, Lizina curtseyed. Alissandra blinked, coming out the door, and then curtseyed as well.

Matteo smiled and bowed to her, taking her hand to pull her back as he straightened himself.

"Have the seamstresses released you?"

Alissandra nodded.

"Then I may show you the gallery, if you choose."

She smiled, and accepted his arm, and Lizina walked discreetly behind, as if she had mastered being a lady-in-waiting at court. The two noblewomen followed after.

The walk was not long. She suspected that some of the nobles who bowed or curtseyed, and withdrew, had intended to walk there them-

selves, and now went off to gossip about how there would be no dancing at the royal wedding.

"I hope you do not find the fitting too arduous."

"It will not last long." She sighed in memory.

"They told a tale about how you once forwent gowns?"

She sighed again. "Once I was sent to buy myself new gowns. I
found a village where they insisted on their rights to have all of a dead
woman's debts paid before they buried her—and worse, a plague had
struck them, and she had spent her money in charity to help, before she
succumbed herself."

His mouth twisted.

"I paid. And went without gowns. And ever after, my parents did
not trust me to clothe myself."

A servant leapt to open the door. Within, there was a vastly long
gallery, with some stretches of empty wall. Beyond there were some
courtiers, far off, who pulled back at their arrival. Alissandra looked
back at the walls. The first two paintings hung were a nuptial painting
of a man and a woman—she detected some resemblance to Matteo—and the painting of a splendid youth, bright-eyed and laughing as
he rode his horse in the forest.

Alissandra's gaze moved between them.

"They took down the portrait done of Sandrino as heir," said Matteo, quietly. "And they were quite glad that Giovanni had consented to
a portrait."

"And there was, no doubt, no time for your portrait?" said Alissandra.

"They sickened so quickly after my brothers died." Matteo's voice
was soft, meditative. "They had expected that Giovanni and even I
would seek our fortunes."

Then he shivered and pointed to the next painting. "Those are my
aunts, with their famed rose tree. The painter took some liberties."

Six comely young women had joined hands in a dance about a rose tree, with only six roses, all as red as the dawn, in full bloom, without a single bud.

"It only put out one rose at a time. And of course, they were not all the same age."

Alissandra's eyebrows went up.

"A lady gave it to my grandparents at their wedding. She said that whenever a daughter was ripe for marriage, she should take the rose that flowered, and throw it into the street. Whichever man took it up would be her bridegroom."

"It must have been a strong enchantment," said Alissandra. "What if he were already married?"

"He never was—or unwilling to wed her, once the surprise faded—though it took longer for each one."

"I would have thought it easier, as the tale spread."

"Ah, but the first one married a king—"

Alissandra nodded.

"The second a prince, the third a duke, the fourth a knight."

Alissandra stared at him.

"The fifth a merchant."

"I can see why the bridegrooms consented, but I wonder at the *brides.*"

"They feared to offend the lady. The sixth—that's Rosalind there—" He pointed at a princess with nut-brown hair streaming to her knees. Alissandra nodded. The princesses could be told from each other, with care, though the likenesses were great. "She waited for years, with the rose blooming on endlessly, not wanting to risk what she guessed would be next. But then my father married."

"Without a rose."

He nodded. "Only with a treaty. And with two women of her generation in the castle—" He studied the portrait. "One day, my grandparents left the castle in the charge of my father and mother. After some days, Rosalind picked the rose and threw it into the street. A rag-and-bone man picked it up. My mother insisted that they had to marry at once."

Alissandra's mouth pursed.

"For fear of the danger to the realm from offending the lady. Of course. So Rosalind went to live in his tumbledown hut." He glanced sideways at her. "One day, she woke up in a golden palace on a hillside."

Alissandra frowned.

"Servants dressed her in silk and in gold, and she had them arrange a great feast. She invited all the great of the city, up to her brother and sister-in-law, and they all come and feasted. While they were eating, her husband came up the road toward the castle, and someone said, 'Look, it's the rag-and-bone man.' Whereupon Rosalind woke up in her own bed.

"The next night, the same thing happened, but the third day, when she invited them, she told them they could come only if they pledged to not refer to her husband as the rag-and-bone man. So, when he came up the road, no one spoke, and when he walked into the castle, he was transformed into a handsome young man, dressed in silk and gold, for he was Prince Guillaume, heir to seven kingdoms, and she had broken the curse on him.

"They waited only for her parents to return, for a grand feast, and then the golden castle bore them off to his own kingdoms and his own parents."

"So, a queen after all." Alissandra shook her head. "My governess told me only of how King Guillaume and Queen Rosalind had seven sons, one for each kingdom. Not what she went through to earn being queen."

Matteo hesitated. "Not only her."

"The one who married a prince?"

His hand swept the air. "Her, no, but my Aunt Violetta, too, who married the merchant."

"I do not know whether to be happy for her," said Alissandra. "Thereby hangs a tale, and tales seldom make those in them happy at the time."

"Then you shall judge. Her husband Antonio taught her all his business, and then set sail on a sea voyage. For three years, he prospered, and was about to sail home again when a great wind blew him far, far, far off course. They were looking for the way back when they found a chest floating on the sea. When they opened it up, they found an enormous golden pearl. Soon after, they found a port, which lay in the kingdom of Queen Sophia."

"Past thrice ten kingdoms and more!" said Alissandra. "Half the scholars of my father's kingdom said she does not exist."

"She existed, at least," said Matteo. "Enough that Antonio presented her with the pearl, which was too grand to sell, and might lure thieves, in order to implore her aid. She gave him a compass that would point the way, a warning that the voyage would take twelve years, and and a choice between a ship full of silver, a ship full of gold, and a ship full of rubies, or—three pieces of advice."

"From Queen Sophia?"

He smiled. "Her first advice was, 'Do not fear what does not threaten harm.' And her second was, 'If you can not see a way out of a problem, consider it again later.' And her third was, 'Do not be quickly angry, do not chop off heads in haste.'

"So he took her advice and sailed. After twelve years, they were in the middle of a vast sea, and out of the water came a great crowd of merfolk and demanded that someone from the ship come to their court. The sailors all feared them, but Antonio saw that they threatened no harm, leapt in the sea, and went with them.

"They bore him deep down under the sea, and when they reached the kingdom on the bottom, they took off a fishy skin, and turned to having legs like landfolk, and led him to their court.

"Now, the king of the merfolk was old, and there was a court case among his kin, and the king told him that he needed someone to judge who was not party to the case, or allied with any of them. So Antonio ruled on the case, and the king declared that since he was so prudent and wise, and the king had no son, Antonio would be his heir and marry whichever of his two young daughters he choose. Now the daughters were as beautiful as the day was long, but Antonio did not know how to refuse them as he was married.

"So he put it off and said that he must settle all his old life, and the king ordered his subjects to aid his return. They swam about the ship and bore it on, and Antonio reached his home port before sundown. He returned to his house and found there Violetta at her dinner making merry with two handsome young men. He was jealous and angry, but he remembered not to chop off heads too soon. So he knocked on the door.

"And when Violetta came to let him in, she shouted, 'Sons! Come quickly! Your father is home!'"

Alissandra laughed. Matteo smiled.

"So they sold up all the business and set sail. And at the king's court, Antonio had his young sons marry the king's daughters, so that they would be heirs after him. And they lived there. Happily ever after."

"In a land beyond where even the boldest merchants sail?"

"Violetta sent word of her grandchildren to her brother and sisters. Some merchants were emboldened to sail there on their pelagic argosies."

She tilted her head to one side, looking at Violetta. "No," she said, "not for me. Even the consolation of two sons would not make amends for a parting of fifteen years. All the troubles of the ball are less than that."

Matteo bowed. "I will note it among my duties, to avoid such storms."

"Your Majesty, Your Highness!" A young seamstress came twittering into the room. She bobbed up and down in a curtsey, without stopping how she spoke of a fitting.

"Before even we have reached my grandparents," said Matteo.

"You shall tell me, come winter, come a rainy day—" She looked down the gallery. There were many, many, many portraits. "We shall have much to keep us occupied. You shall have to tell me all the stories before I have to tell them to our children."

Matteo's mouth twisted into a smile. "Though not after the fitting. Then we must meet with my ministers, to discuss the ambassador to your parents. And our visit to them, after the wedding."

Alissandra stood very still. A state visit, no doubt.

* * *

The morning was still charcoal gray, and not with clouds.

The princess did not rest well at the Princess's Rest, thought Alissandra, looking at the ceiling. Though, did any bride before her wedding?

Half a dozen of the seamstresses descended on the door, urging her to rise.

Just as well. Preparing a bride started as early as baking bread.

* * *

Not just all the servants at the Princess's Rest, but all the village came out to bow her off. Even from the inn, she could see how the entire road was lined with people come to cheer the bridal procession, far more than for the betrothal. The way was as strewn with flowers as if she had combed her hair and washed her hands the length of it, except that there were more than lilies and roses.

Even as she rode on, and on, and the walls of the city appeared ahead of her. Not an inch from the inn to the city did not have its crowds and its flowers.

The city bore more flowers than a garden, and more banners than even for their betrothal. The procession's pace grew ever more stately, but in time, it reached the cathedral. To either side, the nobles gleamed. At the height of the steps stood the archbishop, to preside over the wedding, and the coronation.

And Matteo, regal in royal scarlet, watching her arrive.

Chapter 12

For a floating moment, Alissandra thought she had woken before the dawn, as she had had to when she was a baker, mere weeks ago—but Matteo had already arisen (how quickly she had grown used to it, to notice his absence so swiftly). A second moment brought the susurration of rainfall.

From the window, all the landscape appeared wrapped in silver from the rain. The sounds of movement turned her head back to her husband, and she felt the smile rising on her lips.

"It appears," said Matteo, "that we will not have to wait for winter, to go walking down the gallery."

* * *

Courtiers came down the stairs, making for awkward bows and curtsies, but then, the gallery was where one could walk, sheltered from the rain. They stood aside and were silent. Her mouth twisted. To hear them speak, she had to happen on them—as on the duke who had gravely told his companions that perhaps they were fortunate that the king was not Giovanni, the valiant, but Matteo, the wise and just. She glanced sideways at her husband's face.

At least today he did not have to administer still more justice. She looked ahead, to the gallery.

And once within, Matteo walked past his aunts to the painting of a ball. All the glittering courtiers stood about a handsome young man, dressed as finely as they were, and the lovely young woman whose hand he held, though she was dressed in rags. To one side, looking mischievous, a peasant boy blew on a pipe, with a gaggle of geese about him, and the door behind stood open to the night. The woman had nut-brown hair and looked rather like Matteo, but—

"That's not a proper portrait," said Alissandra.

Matteo chuckled. "No, it is not. No more than the inevitable painting of your dancing with me at the ladies' ball will be. Though here, at
least the painter had seen the scene." He pointed. Near the back of the
crowd, less distinct than the piper, but clearer than most courtiers, sat
the king on his throne.

"My great-grandfather King Giovanni gave a ball so that my grandfather Prince Basil could find a bride, and invited every maiden of suitable birth." His voice was calm and thoughtful.

"There was a nobleman who did not obey him. He had lost all his
kin but his granddaughter Constance, whom he hated because she reminded him of his favorite daughter, her mother. He swore he would
never look on her face, and let her grow up neglected in the corners,
with only her old nurse looking after her, and only a young gooseherd
for her friend. His servants jeered at her, and gave her only scraps for
food and tatters for clothes, while he sat in his room and wept until his
beard grew past his feet, and his tears ran down the stone and etched a
path in it."

She lifted her eyebrows.

"Oh, yes, I have seen it. Beneath that window, nothing green grows.
All killed by salt—but when he got the king's word, he got up and
sent for a barber to sheer off his beard, because he was summoned.
When the old nurse reminded him that his granddaughter was to go,
he cursed her in his fury and declared that she would never go, that she
could die or live as she choose, but never would he bring her.

"She heard this and ran off, weeping, to her friend the gooseherd.
He said to her that they could go to the city where the ball was held and
watched all the people arriving in their finery—that would be a sight.
She did not want to go, but he started to play his pipe, and a bit later,
they were not so much walking as dancing down the road.

"After a time, a finely dressed young man, riding a horse, pulled up
by them and asked if this was the way to the city. They said it was, they
went that way themselves, and so he asked if he might go with them,

and not get lost again, and they all went down the road. The goose-herd piped away, and the finely dressed young man got off his horse and danced along the way with the tattered granddaughter, and when the city came into view, he asked her to marry him.

"She laughed at him, and told him to go to the ball. He'd find many fair and suitable brides then, and forget her utterly.

"He told her that he meant it, and if she came to the ball at mid-night, just as she was, why he would dance with her, just as she was, be-fore all the fine noblemen and noblewomen, and the king himself, and that would show that he truly meant it.

"So, just as midnight struck, she came to the ball, in her tatters, with the gooseherd beside her, and all the dancers tittered. The finely dressed young man was there, even more finely dressed, and stood at the other end of the hall, near the king, but as soon as he saw her, he walked down the length of the room, took her hand, and turned to the king to say, 'Father, this is the woman I wish to marry.'

"And while all the noblewomen hid their smiles behind their fans, the gooseherd lifted his pipe and played a tune, and he vanished with-out a sound, but all her tatters turned to finery."

His hand swept the painting.

"The gooseherd did better by her than the ladies did by me," said Alissandra. "For all the marvelous feathers I gave them."

He laughed a little, under his breath. "I'll show you the gown some-time—her grandfather had to go back to his hall alone, since he had vowed never to look on his granddaughter's face."

"And he's—there still?"

"Died soon after my first aunt was born. And they never saw the gooseherd again, but they lived happily after, and her old nurse was in-stalled in the royal nursery."

A half-smile lingered on his lips, making him look melancholy. "When I was two or three, I toddled one day from the nursery into their chambers—I was something of a favorite with them—my grandmother wished for me that I would find a ball as pleasant to me as theirs had been to them."

For a moment, in the silence, there was only the rain whispering by.

"In the event," said Alissandra, "as well as the result. The second is more important, but—she would not have wished that ball on you."

He nodded. "When I was fourteen, my grandparents made over my great-grandfather's hall to me. She had never set foot in it again, and he never had in the first place, but despite the cobwebs, it is a pleasant enough hall, without her memories."

"Fit for children to frolick in?"

"Very much so."

Rain murmured on the roof. She glanced back at the painting. "I was a bit of a favorite with Aunt Donata—at least, she approved of my sewing."

"Donata." Matteo frowned.

"Not one of my father's three sisters," said Alissandra. "Or my mother's one. In fact, she was, so to speak, my great-grandmother's aunt."

His face cleared. "Queen Rosella's. When King Nicholas married a servant girl."

"So to speak." She smiled. He had not reckoned the years, yet. "She was an orphan, raised by her grandfather, who could not, of course, teach her to spin and weave and sew. When he died, she went into service with the queen mother, who was so fond of her that the other servants grew jealous. They told the queen mother that she had bragged of how she could spin an entire room full of flax in a night, but she had tricked the queen mother into letting her off spinning entirely.

"So Queen Maude had a room filled with flax and ordered her to spin it all in a night, or be executed. It was a heavy stone room in a tower, too, with few windows, and a great stout door, with no manner of escape. Rosella, having nothing better to do, threw herself on the floor of it to weep and wail.

"But at midnight, without the door opening, a little old woman appeared next to her—and she was ugly, ugly, *ugly*. She had eyes as big as saucers, her thumb was as big as a ladle, and she was bent almost double from her hunchback.

"But she kindly asked what was the matter, and when Rosella poured out her story, she said that she would spin it for her if Rosella invited her to the wedding. So Rosella said yes, and all the room hummed as the little old woman spun all the flax into the finest of thread.

"The queen made much of her, even more than before, and gave the thread to the other servants, who were more jealous than before, and then found that they could not even weave the thread, it was so fine. So the servants claimed that she had spun it so it would be useless—only she could weave it.

"Before nightfall, the queen mother had her locked into the tower, and Rosella could weave no more than she could spin, and thought that having rescued her once was already more than she could expect. She wept again, but the little old woman appeared again. This time, she said that she must have her sit among the high table, among the high guests, and Rosella agreed, and she wove it all.

"The queen mother was pleased, but the seamstresses were not. They were more jealous than ever of her favor, and the cloth was so fine and delicate that they could not sew it. So they told the queen mother that she had woven it so it would be useless, only she could weave it.

"Before nightfall, the queen mother had her locked into the tower again, and told her to make two shifts of it, one for herself, and one for her bridegroom, the king, for no dowry was better than skill at spinning, weaving, and sewing, and her industry would serve them well. Rosella could sew no more than she could spin or weave, and she wept again. But the little old woman came again, and told her she would sew it all up, on the condition that Rosella call her 'Aunt' on the day of her wedding.

"Now Rosella realized she had already promised that this little old woman would sit at the high table at the king's wedding. But she agreed, and the little old woman sewed up the finest shifts that ever were seen. The queen mother ordered the rest of the wedding clothes made, and King Nicholas was pleased because Rosella was very beautiful.

"But when the wedding feast was all set out with dishes, the little old woman walked in, and if she had been ugly by night, she was uglier still by day. Rosella leapt up from her seat to say, 'Aunt! You must sit at the high table at my wedding feast!'

"The little old woman laughed and chortled and admired the fineness of their garments, the luxury of the dishes, and the manners of the bridegroom, who did not ask the question he wished to ask—but she would bait him until he spoke, and so he blushed but asked how his lovely bride had such an ugly aunt.

"The little old woman assured him that once she had been fully as lovely as Rosella, but she was always spinning, and weaving, and sewing. Her thumb's so big because she held the flax, spinning and spinning and spinning. Her back's so bent because she's always leaning over the loom, weaving and weaving and weaving. Her eyes are so big because she stared at the cloth at night, sewing and sewing and sewing—"

She paused. Matteo lifted an eyebrow.

"So King Nicholas forbade his bride to ever spin or weave or sew again."

Matteo's laughter cracked from him. "That was a better garment from the ladies than the ones you were given—but how can you know this tale? She would not have told."

"She would not have while Queen Maude lived. But after their daughter Helena was born—after the queen mother died—she confessed all. By that point, King Nicholas found it as mirthful as you did."

He nodded, gravely.

"And you will meet Aunt Donata on our visit, at my parents' castle."

Matteo paused. She could almost hear him counting the years. He nodded. There was a lady not afraid to let it be known what she was.

A gust sent raindrops splattering against the window.

"You must have tales of these portraits that make a person question how the tale could be known." Then she could have bit her tongue, remembering his brothers.

Matteo did not seem to recall that tale. He looked down the corridor and said, slowly. "Not really, not here." His voice took up briskly. "Though on my mother's side, there was her father. His name was True."

Her mouth pursed. Her governesses had mentioned such a prince.

"And his brother's name was Untrue. Named for their natures. One day they set out to seek their fortunes. Once they had eaten half their food, Untrue stole all of True's, and told him he had eaten it in the night. Well, True was hungry, not full, and saw how Untrue's bag was full up, though it had been half empty the night before.

"So True said, 'Well you were named, Untrue by name and untrue by nature.'

"At that his brother flew at him, put out his eyes, and left him in the woods to perish."

Alissandra swallowed. At least Esmeralda and Iolande had done nothing like that.

"By fumbling about with his hands, True found a tree and climbed it for safety. Now, it was St. John's Eve, and three animals met beneath the tree—a bear, a fox, and a hare."

At which point it struck her, coldly, that if Matteo himself had escaped unscathed, his brother had not fared so well.

"The bear asked what news they had. It itself had learned that the dew that formed beneath the tree was a sovereign remedy for every form of blindness.

"And the fox said that it had learned that the king of the Red Castle was trying to dig a well, and would have no luck because of the golden chain buried beneath the great oak tree. If that were dug up, he would have no need for a well, because a great spring would rise up and give him enough water for seven castles.

"And the hare said that it had learned the king's daughter was mute, but that was because an enemy had put five swan's feathers in her pillow. If he knew to fill the pillows with fresh goose feathers, she would speak as well as ever she did.

"The bear said they had all spent their year profitably, and would meet again the next year.

"When the beasts were gone, True waited only until he heard the birds singing for the dawn, to climb down and gather the dew. No sooner had he washed his eye sockets with the dew than he could see better than ever. So he went on his way, and came to the king's castle, where he took service—as Untrue had taken before him.

"Untrue's heart grew bitter as soon as he saw True alive and well, and he feared whatever magic had let him regain his sight. So he went to the king and told him that True had bragged that he could get the king a good well. The king summoned True and said he must do as he bragged of. He would be richly rewarded for success, but his head would be cut off if he failed.

"True bowed low and told the king he needed men to dig. He set the men to dig up the gold chain at the root of the oak, and no sooner had they done so that a spring welled up.

"The king gave him ten times more gold than the chain, but said he would rather have his daughter speak again than have seven wells. So True told him to change her pillows. The king declared that if it worked, he should marry her, and had the pillows changed.

"But as soon as the princess could speak, she declared she would not marry a sorcerer whatever her father promised, and so she would not marry True unless he told how he knew these things. So True told them his tale. Untrue, hearing that True had told of his attack, fled, and since it was nearly St. John's Eve again, went to that tree.

"The beasts gathered again, and the bear said that someone had spied on them last year and learned their secrets. This year, before they told their news, they would find any spy and deal with him as he deserved. They found Untrue up the tree, and tore him to pieces."

Silence fell, except for the splatter of rain. A gust rattled a window.

"So," said Alissandra dryly, "how did they hear of his death?"

"A royal servant had come to spy as well, and brought back news," said Matteo. "He claimed he had just happened by, and the king elected to act as if he believed him. It did discourage other spies."

She smiled. "I wonder if they were lords or ladies, those beasts."

He shrugged. "Could be. But there are other things that cause strangeness."

"Your Majesty, Your Majesty!" A page pelted up. "Your Majesty, there are petitioners!"

Matteo's shoulders slumped.

Alissandra touched his arm. "It has to be important, to have come in such weather."

"Or, they think it so," said Matteo, gloomily.

Chapter 13

Three glorious days, thought Alissandra, as she stood beneath the arched doorway to the courtyard. Brilliant and flowery. One for her betrothal, one for her wedding and coronation, and one for the day they set out toward her father's kingdom.

The ambassador from her parents had been formally correct in every respect. So was their own company. She could not remember her parents ever having such a retinue, even when they visited another sovereign.

Then, whomever her parents had visited, they had not come as a runaway from that place, returning.

And the longer they lingered, Alissandra told herself, the longer she had to dread it.

Her gaze drifted to where Lizina had already mounted her horse. She had graciously declined Matteo's offer to grant her a title. She remained a servant at the castle, but at least a servant, as well as a noblewoman, could attend her.

Matteo appeared beside her. "Ready?" He had a little half-smile, and she felt her lips curve. At least she would not be alone.

* * *

Tents stood like a forest about the inn. Erected with the haste of men long familiar with housing themselves so.

The grooms still took their horses, since she and Matteo and even some servants would stay in the Princess's Rest. Of course.

She looked up at the building. Would her parents' castle seem as unsettling? Beside her, Matteo spoke in a low voice to a stableboy.

"Oh yes," said the boy brightly. "They're full of stories. There's a swamp along the way—"

Alissandra turned toward them.

144

"—and there's this hag lady in it." The boy rubbed his nose with the back of his hand. "Some of them say she's always been there, nobody's noticed, but everyone can see her now." He lowered his voice. "'cause it smells *horrible*. All the time. It stinks. Nothing like a swamp." He shook his head. "They said she boasted about two captive princesses, but no one's seen 'em, 'cause no one wants to stay that long."

Lizina came up and curtseyed to give them news of dinner.

* * *

The next day, as they rode, Lizina observed, without taking her gaze from the road's duty, "A lady can use a curse to hold someone."

"What, not just curse someone so he can not leave?" said Alissandra.

Lizina's mouth twitched in a smile. "There are often strange bounds to their powers to curse. But they can make a curse a tangible thing, and keep the person bound by it."

"Until the person finds it again," said Alissandra, slowly, "like a swan maiden." Though, usually, she had help from her children, Alissandra remembered.

"That lasts for years, usually," said Lizina. "Long enough for it to be trouble." Her mouth twisted. "Your great-great-grandfather was uncommonly prudent, and you see she needed his aid."

"Still, the lady would have to guard it carefully to prevent that," said Matteo. "The swan maiden's cloak, among those foolish enough to hold her captive, is always well-hidden."

"Oh, very carefully," said Lizina. "Still, for a curse like those on your sisters, if you break the thing, they are free of the curse."

"If you find it," said Matteo. "And how would you?" He thought for a moment. "If she checked whether it was, perhaps."

"And who would need to check?" said Alissandra. "Esmeralda could not be quite that long. The lady could always *smell* that they were there." Because nothing could cover up that smell.

And then she felt cold. Nothing. Except one thing.

* * *

Trees towered from the dark earth, and made it darker with their shadows. The pools could be told more by their smoothness than by any glint of light; they came up to the very brink of the muddy path. The horses' fetlocks were covered in mud, and in their path, hoof-shaped puddles formed.

The smell crept up on them, on top of the moldering plants, but even so it did not inure their noses. The unmistakable stench—

"How can any woman, even a hag, stand to live in this reek?" said Matteo.

"Your noses get used to stenches," said a courtier, obsequiously.

Alissandra shook her head. "You think of the ordinary sort of stenches, good sir. Such as a nose might get used to. But this is a curse laid by a lady. You would smell it forever."

"What is that to us?" said a squire. "Do travelers go down that path? Is it worth troubling a lady who will harm no passerby?"

"If I could know that," said Matteo, "indeed, she would not be worth troubling. But that I can not know."

* * *

For a path so seldom used, it was in uncommonly good repair.

"Your Majesties!" called a rider. "There's a mist behind us!"

Alissandra turned, quickly. Mist had risen, milky white and flooding the forest behind them.

"With that," murmured Matteo, "how could they know she would harm no passer-by?" He reached out to take her hand.

The stench was stronger.

"If that's—Esmeralda—" whispered Alissandra.

Matteo nodded.

Alissandra, smiling a little, produced a comb with her other hand. Matteo smiled, but said, "Not yet."

She nodded.

* * *

The cottage was low, ramshackle: the roof sagged, and moss overgrew most of it. The picket fence slumped, even to the ground in places, though it was hard to pick out for all the rank weeds that thronged around the pickets.

The garden, for all its tangles and lack of flower beds, burst with flowers and herbs that any witch would treasure, even if the smell of them was utterly muffled in the stench. She flinched a little when she saw the deadly nightshade and the other poisons, but her gaze went on.

Beside the cottage, two young women, wearing drab rags, knelt on the earth and picked leaves. One grumbled in a low voice, but not until Matteo and Alissandra reached the fence did they look up. The faces were so weary and worn that Alissandra registered that with shock before she could look past it and be sure that they were her sisters.

"You!" Filthiness bubbled from Esmeralda's mouth. "You gloating tyrant!"

Alissandra let out her breath.

"Tyrant!" said Iolande.

Alissandra drew out her comb again, tilted her head to one side, and combed her free-falling hair. Roses fell, flowering, and the scent decreased.

"Show off! Come to gloat that you do not share our affliction!"

"Affliction!"

Slowly, Matteo freed her hand. He dismounted, and walked up to Iolande. Alissandra dismounted to trail behind him, spreading roses along the way.

"Have you any water?" he said. "Can you show me where it is?"

Iolande looked blankly at him, neither pointing nor shaking her head. Matteo sighed, looked about, and walked over to a clump of rocks—where a pitcher sat. Alissandra followed. Water bubbled among the rocks. She put aside the comb, and held out her hands. Matteo poured water over them, cold from the spring, but as she rubbed her hands together, lilies sprung up.

"So *your* nose is too pretty to suffer." Esmeralda's lip curled for a moment of blessed silence—but only a moment. "Leave your own blood sisters to suffer, but your light of love—he's too precious."

"Too precious," said Iolande, somehow managing to infuse contempt into her sad little voice.

Alissandra tossed back her hair and shook the water from her hands. "I will not leave. Even if you ask courteously."

For once, Esmeralda was shocked into silence.

Then Matteo's hand settled on Alissandra's, and he steered her into the shadows of green behind the well. There, she picked out the hag bent over her staff and muttering.

The lady, she reminded herself. Rudeness would be unwise. Her mouth twitched. Including the rudeness of letting it be known that she realized that this old hag was a lady.

The hag stomped to the middle of the garden. There, she stopped. She sniffed. After a moment, she sniffed again.

Slowly, her head turned, her rheumy eyes shifting to take in the garden. Her gaze passed over Iolande and Esmeralda. Esmeralda looked sullenly and resentful but, at least, did not blurt out where Matteo and Alissandra were. Iolande wrung her hands helplessly.

Softly, hoarsely, the hag said, "It can't be." Her voice grew harsher and louder. "It can't be!" She stamped off another way, faster than she had moved before.

Her heart hammering out the moments, Alissandra joined Matteo in hurrying after, into the thickets of trees behind the huts. The path was not even very muddy, and the hag was so bent on the way that they easily followed.

At a hollow tree, the hag thrust her hand into the shadowy gap. Her fingers, shaking a little, pulled out two cords, both knotted.

For a moment, all was still. Alissandra scarcely dared to breathe. The curse catchers.

The hag smiled a little. "So that's all—" Then she scowled. "But why—" She edged a little away from the tree, into greater light, eyed the cords again, and turned back toward the path.

Matteo, his knife already in hand, strode the distance between them. The hag gaped. He snatched the cords from her hand, grabbed all four ends, and sliced them through the middle.

"You—you—!" The hag started to expand in size, as if her rage, unable to find words, was bursting out in other ways. "You *thief*!"

Matteo scrambled back. Alissandra turned before him and fled. Branches seemed to leap out and snag, but she blundered through, with Matteo on her heels, and burst out into the garden. Her sisters gaped at her.

"Come!" she said.

For once, Esmeralda had no words. Alissandra grabbed Iolande and hustled her along the path away. Esmeralda collected her wits enough to follow, with Matteo behind them and the mists fading before them. They reached their white-faced company faster than she could have imagined possible.

"Horses for my sisters," called Matteo. "Or—" He glanced at them again. "A cart if they can not ride."

* * *

"You can not count on our father's blessing," said Iolande, with uncommon poison in her voice. "Let alone half the kingdom now and all after he dies. You know what he meant."

She looked about the landscape, full of rich farmlands and orchards heavy with unripe fruit. Greedily, thought Alissandra.

"That's our father's decision," said Alissandra, firmly.

"O, his blessings might be yours," said Esmeralda, sweetly, as she rode up beside Alissandra. "Quite certainly. After all, *I'm* not going to marry a king who thinks *you* any kind of worthy princess."

Iolande giggled. "Any kind of worthy princess," she said, low voiced, and then spoke more loudly. "I would not marry him either."

"It's unlucky to talk like that," said Lizina, gravely. Iolande and Esmeralda gave her poisonous glares. "If ill fortune befell your sister, some might say that you cast an evil eye on her."

The looks grew more poisonous.

Alissandra wondered how short they could cut the visit. She was a queen now and had to consider the well-being of her own kingdom and own subjects even more than she had the well-being of her father's subjects (as long as it did not involving sacrificing the money meant for her gowns). Though she did have to weigh the consequences of causing offense.

Certainly nothing else about the visit would lure her to stay an hour more than they needed.

Chapter 14

Esmeralda's face was turning red, and an unbecoming shade of red at that. "Us. It was to be us, with half the kingdom as a dowry for the one who chose one of the princesses he rescued as a bride."

"Certainly," said Matteo coldly, "if your father *wishes* to break his word, my patrimony is quite sufficient for myself and my bride."

Esmeralda looked ready to scream.

"My child," said King Frederick, "I read the proclamation most carefully. You know it does not go well when a king tries to add conditions after he dislikes how it turns out. He always suffers as a consequence. He's lucky if he ends up looking like a fool after he kissed a donkey. He could end up magically bound to ferry travelers—or *dead*." He waved a hand in the air. "And there are other ways to win you a bridegroom. We could sit you on a glass mountain with golden apples in your lap and marry you off to the knight who managed to reach you and take them." He frowned. "Perhaps I should not marry you off to the first passer-by, that is unreliable, and unpleasant for the princess, but we may have to resort to it—"

Matteo glanced at Alissandra. How unfair of him. It was hard enough already to keep from laughing.

"Or just have the young men line up and have you and Iolande each hand one a golden apple." Then he blinked. "But first of all, we shall hold a feast to honor my new son and confirm him and his bride to receive the kingdom after my death, out of gratitude that you and Iolande were safely delivered from captivity."

Esmeralda looked thunderous.

Donata poked her head in the door and hooted with laughter. "You need to get yourself distressed again, o princess. A captive of horrible monsters. Only then can some other man rescue you!"

Esmeralda's mouth tightened, visibly holding back words.

Matteo glanced at Donata and to Alissandra, and she wished she could speak to tell him that was, indeed, the Donata she had told him of.

Once we are out, she told herself.

"Now, don't be silly, Donata," said King Frederick. "Trolls and dragons do not kidnap young princesses merely because one wishes it."

* * *

Alissandra sat on the bed, and sewed. Her mother eyed the shirt in her lap.

"This is for my husband," Alissandra said, mildly. In due course, she would have to find an orphanage or the like in Matteo's kingdom, but for now—she smiled a little—as a bride she could replenish Matteo's wardrobe.

From the doorway, Donata snorted. And then swept in with queenly dignity, despite her shortness, her ugliness, and her drab clothes.

"Certainly no one will complain of you, Your Majesty," she said. "Did all you should and ended up well."

"I had some help," said Alissandra. Donata eyed Lizina—a little oddly, thought Alissandra—before she turned on Iolande and Esmeralda.

"But you two! How could you have been such fools? Letting that hag catch you!"

Esmeralda pulled back as if she had seen a snake.

"It was a trap," said Iolande, plaintively. "She asked us to get some wool, and it was golden, and the sheep *breathed fire.*"

Esmeralda nodded. "That's not something anyone should be expected to face—"

"Except you didn't need to," said Donata. "If you had *listened* instead of riding off during your lessons, you would have known to look for wool caught in brambles." She snorted. "If you have brought your wits, you would have looked about and seen it for yourself. You're lucky she wanted maidservants and not meat."

She turned to Queen Olivia. "Your Majesty, let them come to the countryside to learn wisdom, or at least sense. It is not like it would do them a lick of good to set out to seek their fortunes if they stay fools."

* * *

People moved about slowly on the foggy day. Alissandra and Matteo slipped down corridors without meeting more than servants slipping off about their business.

At the gallery door, Donata stumped out of the room. She eyed them, smiled, and stood aside to let them in. Alissandra's mouth twisted, but Matteo merely nodded to Donata.

The daylight was dim, but candles were set about, and all the portraits glowed with color.

Matteo picked out the first. "That is the tale you told at the inn," he said. "Jean the king's godson, and the mangy man."

"At the very moment he was unmasked." Alissandra nodded. "This is my mother's grandparents—my parents are fourth cousins, so we have some from her family paintings—with the famous oranges."

"I heard of the canary," said Matteo, glancing sideways at her.

"It's one thing to sneak into a witch's lair, prudently giving gifts to her servants so they will let you escape with three enchanted oranges. It's another to foolishly leave your beloved where another witch can conjure her back into a canary, and fool you into thinking she's your beloved, bewitched. No, he did not much like that part of the tale. . . ." Her gaze went on. "There's King Nicholas, and Queen Rosella, and the one past them is King Christopher, and Queen Maleen."

"And the source of the two kingdoms?" said Matteo.

"O, you heard that?"

"Some," said Matteo. "I might not have heard it all." He gave her sideways glance.

She laughed. "Prince Nicholas and Princess Maleen were the children of neighboring kingdoms, both only children. Her father did not want them to marry, so he immured her in a great tower with a servant for seven years, with food enough for that, and thought that would cure her of such nonsense. When the seven years were nearly up, they realized that no one was coming to break them out, so they tried to burrow out.

"When they succeeded, they found themselves in a land ravaged by war. Cottages burned to the ground, orchards cut down, domestic beasts driven off or eaten, wild beasts hunted until none remained, fields rank with weeds. She and the maid fled, but they ate thistles and nettles before they escaped the realm—and after, too, because they kept trying to enter service and being refused. Only when they reached the king's castle were they taken on, and then as scullery maids.

"Now, this was the land of Prince Christopher's father, King Leandro, who had just insisted that his son be betrothed, and Prince Christopher had told him that since he would not see his beloved Princess Maleen again, she could not have escaped that war alive, he was willing to do his duty."

Matteo raised an eyebrow.

"And the bride was distantly related to Princess Maleen, but very ugly. The day of her wedding, she ordered the scullery maid, as she thought her, to dress up in her wedding gown and go to the church, so no one would see how ugly she was until the wedding was over.

"But at the wedding, Prince Christopher put a necklace about her neck, as token that she was his true bride, and when she went back, the ugly bride tried to take it away, and it would not come. So the ugly bride said to the guards that she was an imposter and witch, and they should execute her at once.

"As the guards tried to drag her off, the prince and the king came to see what delayed the bride, and Prince Christopher said, seeing his scullery maid without her veil, that if he had not known it was impossible, he would have thought her Princess Maleen.

"Princess Maleen told him that she was, and what had happened, and King Leandro had the ugly bride's head cut off for trying to kill her, and she and Prince Christopher lived happily ever after."

She looked down the gallery. Their children would have to learn these, as well, but a page boy ran toward the galley. She sighed and turned back. There were festivities, no doubt.

* * *

Tales had reached even here. The masquers, having changed from silver, now danced before the thrones and about the hall in gold, in honor of Queen Alissandra's brave rescue of King Matteo.

If the room was not half so splendid as the original dancing hall, neither of those who knew that minded in the least. Matteo, if anything, looked a little smug at the measures that he did not have to join.

Fresh-faced maidens curtseyed, and bright-eyed youths bowed, and both groups swept from the floor to be replaced by flame-clad dancers. A drably clad servant tried to pick his way about. It took Alissandra a minute to realize that he headed for the thrones, through the crowd, but then she scowled and took the arm of a page to whisper an order.

As the boy trotted off, she sat back and hoped it was not a dragon, there being no good news good enough to bring a servant to interrupt. It would be ill news, but waiting would not improve it.

With the page's livery opening the way, the servant was soon on one knee before them, recounting how soldiers had seen Princess Esmeralda riding away toward the border.

Matteo started. Alissandra glanced about. Indeed, she had not seen her since—since the banquet. How much it must have angered her, that she could escape without the slightest notice of anyone in court.

Iolande sat with her hands in her lap, and looked pale, angry, and betrayed. At least, thought Alissandra, she would not be able to ape her in this.

"However—insolent her reasoning," said King Frederick, "I see no reason to interrupt the feast. It is not in her honor, and often she has gone on long rides to cool her temper."

"But, consider, my dear!" said Queen Olivia, "the danger! Who knows how hard the hag will resent her escape?"

A councilor cleared his throat. "It is an insult to King Matteo to let his boldness be put to naught by her insolence."

Her parents blinked as if this were the first point at which they thought it had something to do with their royal guests.

Matteo shifted his weight, but bit down any words. Finally King Frederick gave orders for soldiers to search for the princess—but for the festivities to go on.

And, Alissandra conceded, most of the revelers would be useless in a search.

* * *

The sunset was pure gold when, from the front door, the riders came into sight, riding back. A brisk enough pace, but they were not riding as if they looked for aid. Not only did they have no one among their number who looked like Esmeralda, one of them led a rider-less horse.

Her gaze searched out Matteo, who looked grave and reflective. Her father's ordering it to continue had not maintained the mood of the feast. And it had taken heroic effort to avoid waspishly observing that Esmeralda had managed to divert the court's attention from the honored guests to herself.

One rider, in the courtyard, handed off the reins to a stable boy and mounted the stairs, to go on one knee before King Frederick and Queen Olivia.

His voice was very formal. "Your Majesties. The Princess Esmeralda rode far—very hard, and very far. Even to the famed ferry, where the ferryman must bear passengers until such time as one is foolish enough to let him jump out, and then he is free, and the passenger is the new ferryman."

Silence fell. Alissandra thought that, perhaps, he should actually speak of how Esmeralda was now the ferryman.

"Impossible," said Queen Olivia, but she looked as white as snow. "That tale is too well known, and our bold, brave Princess Esmeralda would not let anyone thus—"

King Frederick raised his hand. Queen Olivia fell silent.

"The old ferryman?" he said.

"We did not find him. Villagers spoke of an old man and how he babbled of being a merchant, of his wealth, and of how his fool daughter would lavish it on a peasant's son."

"Too late," whispered Alissandra. Matteo glanced at her. She stepped closer. "All his wealth was lost at sea by his grandson. His great-granddaughter Catherine had to go into service, she was so poor." She glanced at him. "Though she ended up a queen—and my mother's grandmother."

"Let us hope that some kind soul will take him in," said Matteo. After a minute, he added, "It is the law of the land here that after seven years thus trapped, you are dead at law?"

Alissandra nodded.

* * *

In their ante-chamber the next dawn, as they readied themselves to see Iolande off, a servant scurried in.

She had barely time to tell them that Donata had arrived, declaring she had to see to Iolande in the country, and could not return for their departure, but she had to see Matteo and Alissandra again, when the lady herself stomped in. The bundle in her arms was enormous, the cloth showing black.

"A present for newly-weds," said Donata cheerfully. The bundle took a minute for them to unfold. Great, vast curtains of midnight black with stars glittering in them. A magnificent array, from the most bright to the most dim.

Easier to carry that some of the gifts they had been given, thought Alissandra, and tried not to think on why Donata had chosen this one.

She laid it aside. She could add it to the dowry chest and the other things she was bringing. First they had to see Iolande off.

* * *

The morning was more gray than pink or yellow, but the tiny company gathered nonetheless. Donata was cheerful and said that hardship built character, Iolande could learn how Alissandra was better off for being a baker for a year. Iolande was meek and silent, barely responding even to her parents and sister.

Then they rode off.

King Frederick cleared his throat. "Your Majesty," he said to Matteo. "We must settle on half the kingdom, on a map, before you can depart."

Matteo nodded gravely, and offered Alissandra his arm.

The map had already been cut in two, and it offered no surprises. True, for generations the kingdom had not been joined to another by matrimony; even a princess such as her mother had not brought a kingdom as dowry. But her father's mother's father's mother had indeed been Princess Maleen, and if the border forest had been dissolved by the wedding, it was there to rise again.

Not so strongly as between her parents' kingdom and Matteo's, she reminded herself, since she and Matteo would inherit the rest. Half regrown, no more than to indicate the border, though enough to make merchants grumble—if her governesses' histories were accurate.

But however it grew or did not, by law, she and Matteo were the sovereigns of Maleen's old kingdom. Without even its needing to be subdued again after the war; it had grown prosperous. Since it bordered Matteo's, that border forest would thin; she doubted that any merchant would even think of that as counter-balancing this loss.

"The old royal castle has never been rebuilt," said her father.

Matteo nodded. He had, after all, had tutors as well.

"But you have your own castle and do not need another. And Alissandra will, of course, remember parts of it."

For a moment, Alissandra could not breathe. He—he could not—he smirked. She forced her breath out. Whatever unkindness he said, he had not chosen it because it contained the village; between the castle and the border, it was the only reasonable half to give them.

Matteo's face was set like flint. Her father talked of the taillage that was owed—and waived—whenever a new king reigned. And how they had to go on a progress through their new land. Best if they did it from this castle to their own.

Alissandra looked at the map, the journey laid out there, going through that village. Her mouth tightened. She would visit the grave-yard where that woman lay.

Her father said, "We should proclaim that the taillage had been waived as you set out."

"No," said Matteo. "It must be proclaimed in the kingdom that will enjoy it."

Her mother and her father blinked.

When they withdrew to their chamber, Alissandra asked, "Would his clerks draw up the proclamation that you mean to utter?"

"Oh, no," said Matteo. "At least, so I hope. But I must do nothing against the law, when it is my place to uphold it."

"You are thinking of something," said Alissandra.

He nodded. "Thinking of laws." His mouth twisted. "I do not think they could learn to fear your justice, but they might fear mine."

He ran a hand through his hair. "It would be best if we arrived after the haying was done."

Her mouth twisted. These were her subjects now, and it would be madness to begrudge the peasants that time. It would not keep them here much longer, she told herself.

Chapter 15

After the scything of the hay meadows, the summer still burned hot. Harvest ripened in the fields, and ditches blazed with wildflowers in full bloom. At every village and almost every crossroads, peasants came to greet them, with garlands of flowers, or masques where the performers smeared their faces with charcoal and wore one another's clothes for costume, or danced to instruments, or sang. It often took them three or four days to cover a day's journey.

He did not proclaim that he waived the taillage.

After a week, on a day where they had passed only one village before, Alissandra looked ahead to where orchards stood, and her mouth went dry. The trees were no longer showering white petals like snowfall, but bearing ripening and full-ripe fruit. Still, it was the orchard.

Matteo pulled up his horse. "This is the village?"

She nodded.

He let out his breath and surveyed it, as if actually facing it was a shock, but as their road wound through the orchard, his face set. The chapel appeared ahead, with the graves beyond, and no lit candles to indicate a body lay there.

Then the villagers emerged. They wore their best, they bore garlands, and few smirked as they looked at her.

Matteo's gaze flickered from one smirk to the next, and his mouth set as if he had come to a decision. He looked sternly over them and raised his voice.

"Of this village, I have heard much. Her Majesty has told me how zealous you are, for your rights."

More of them smirked, and more broadly.

He smiled back, without its reaching his eyes. "I, too, am zealous of my rights."

The smirks slackened, a bit, among the wiser souls. Alissandra's heart started to hammer, not faster, but harder, in her chest. She forced her breath in and out, to keep calm, and to look regal.

Matteo's gaze traveled over the crowd. "You come with flowers in hand, and not the taillage that is my due."

Alissandra's breath gushed out. The villagers stared at Matteo as if he had treacherously stabbed them.

Be yourself—she said, as dispassionately as she could manage, "That would be twenty-fold of the debts I paid here."

Matteo lifted an eyebrow. "Then I would be twenty times a fool to forgo it."

She nodded. He did not look for a pretext for pardon, then.

"For all the other villages in the kingdom, and all the towns and cities, I pronounce full remittance of the taillage for every corporation willing to renounce the right to withhold burial for the dead whose debts can not be paid. Those who wish to maintain that right will pay in full all taillage and any other duty, whomever else I remit it for."

For a moment, it looked as if the villagers had turned to stone.

She kept her own face unmoving; it did not become a queen to gawk like a country chit. Their own company seemed as startled, except for Lizina, whose face was the implacable mask that Alissandra strove for.

"You may hope for the remittance of duties to come," said Matteo. "But not this one."

* * *

Late at night, with the inn chamber lit only by two candles, a maid-servant combed out Alissandra's hair. Matteo entered. His mouth was fixed, and the candlelight cast more shadows than light across his face.

The maid laid aside the comb, curtseyed, and withdrew. the door snicked shut behind her.

"I will make the taillage over to you," he said, his voice hollow. "You don't have to spend it all on dresses—you don't have to spend any of it on dresses—but you must take it."

Alissandra swallowed. "I could—" How thin her voice was—she tried to force more strength into it. "—spend it all on clothes for orphans. Hire a dozen seamstress for a year or two."

He nodded slowly.

* * *

Villages, towns, cities all hastened to assure King Matteo and Queen Alissandra of their delight in renouncing so odious a right, as their progress continued to the border.

They passed by the ruined tower where Princess Maleen had been captive. Vast blocks of stone could just be made out beneath the ivy, with trees towering around it. What still stood was lower than many of those trees. Within half a day's journey, Alissandra pointed out where the castle had stood. It lay in ruins so utter that only her lessons let her see it.

She was glad when the line of trees that marked the border appeared ahead of them. Though the changes in the forest could be marked at quite a distance.

"I do not think we shall meet another hag," she said.

"Woodcutters, on the other hand—" Matteo shook his head.

* * *

The Princess's Rest was as bustling as she remembered it, and still all the servants came out to bow and curtsey. To Alissandra's surprise, a handsome young man bowed beside Bernardo as if he were all but master here. Carla, looking smug, made her curtsey standing next to him.

Ushering to the royal chambers gave no time for questions, but minutes after, Lizina opened the door to let Bernardo in.

He put a tray of bread and butter and jam on the table, and a jug of cider. "It is good to see you again, even if we have been so abustle with commonplace guests."

"What," said Matteo, "has kept you so distracted?"

"Perhaps Your Majesty may remember my son Danilo? I hope not, he was a scamp. One day he went to seek his fortune, and went to work as a merchant's cook. The merchant lost a ring. He promised that whoever found it would get the captaincy of one of his ships. And one day my son served him a fish, and he found the ring inside it.

"Now, he had no wish to let a cook be a captain, so he took an old wreck, manned it with ancient soldiers, and filled it with salt for cargo, and sent my son out into the teeth of a storm. They were blown far, far, far away, and they found an island where all the food was savorless, because they had no salt. He sold his cargo for a shipload of fine gems, sailed back, and took his captain's share, and returned home with it."

"That tale must have kept you all busy listening for a while," said Alissandra.

"That it did," said Bernardo. "But then they had a dance to welcome him back, and a dark-haired dancer appeared out of nowhere, dressed in a gown like all the clouds in the sky."

Alissandra stilled. Matteo looked grave, and she blinked; true, she had not told him the tale.

"Such as merchants might sell, not as a lady might conjure. She was lovely enough that Danilo danced with no one else, and when she flitted off again at the end, he was heart-broken.

"But when he took to his bed, Carla offered to make him a bread pudding. And no sooner had she brought it in—and her all covered with flour—than he said that she looked very like the lovely dancer at the dance.

"She laughed at him and said she was just a lowly baker, but he recovered all the same and insisted on another dance. The lovely dancer came again, in a gown like all the flowers in the field, but she ran off again. And Danilo had a ring commissioned, all pretty and delicate, and had us have a third dance. This time, he slipped the ring on her finger, and the next day took to his bed, and asked her to bring a bread pudding. She did, but he caught her wearing the ring."

"And she yielded," said Alissandra, meditatively, taking a slice of bread and jam.

"It brought her around, apparently. She was blushing like the morn when she admitted it. She agreed to marry him."

"Good fortune for the bride and bridegroom," said Matteo, lifting his cup. Then he sat back, murmuring, "Pretending not to be herself. . . ."

Alissandra nodded. "She left home because her father once did not recognize her."

Both men blinked.

"She told me and Lizina, in order to persuade us that she knew how to keep a secret. She was the only other one to know that—I was trying to rescue you."

* * *

At the window, golden leaves flooded by, on a gust of autumnal wind. Golden as—

Her own hair, thought Alissandra firmly. It was hard to turn her thought away from wishes for the child. But even to wish that the child would have hair like her own was unwise.

She let her hand rest on her waist.

"Your Majesty," said Lizina, "we do have a large set of clothes for the poor."

A welcome distraction, thought Alissandra.

* * *

Snowflakes drifted down, one by one, past leafless boughs, to melt on the brown, bare earth. The baby kicked. Alissandra leaned on the window frame.

"What grave thoughts are you thinking?" said Matteo, coming up beside her.

"Of the folly of promises." She glanced sideways at her. "If I ever ask you to always do what the child asks of you, or to never remarry except to a woman as lovely as I am, or one who could wear something of mine, or to make sure the stepmother does not take charge of my child by having him raised in a tower—I should ask you to promise that you would take either one as delirium."

His smile was strained. "You could ask me to never marry again except to a great princess."

She blinked. "*What*? Why would—" She shook her head. "So many miller's daughters and gardener boys were honorable monarchs."

"The purported reason was so that becoming a queen would not turn her head."

"Did it work?"

"Alas, the king's courtiers, searching for a bride, found a woman who claimed she had been a queen, and had been driven from her husband's land—with her daughter—by the army that killed him. They were fools to trust her."

"Ah. She should have asked him to never marry a bride whose past he did not know for certain."

Matteo smiled.

"One of your ancestresses?" she said.

"No, but my oldest aunt, the one who married a king—it was a tale of his ancestors—the king had both a son and daughter by his first marriage."

"Perhaps we should go to the gallery," she said, "and hear more tales of yours."

He offered her his arm.

"Your Majesties." By the door, a servant bowed. "A message from El-ferrin." She straightened. A letter in her hand bore a regal seal.

Matteo stepped over and took it. Opening it revealed that Iolande had vanished. Just left one day without returning. Alissandra felt cold.

"I hope the wolves did not eat her. Though perhaps without Esmeralda leading her into folly, she might actually find her fortune."

"Let us hope that she does not end up married to a cobbler as a condition of being disenchanted," said Matteo.

* * *

Snow fell. And fell. And fell. The air outside was still, so it did not swirl, but it blanketed field and forest and cottage and castle.

Snug within a room hung with green, and warm with fire and candle, Alissandra lay in her bed and admired the solemn, staring infant swaddled beside her. At the door, Lizina was speaking in a low voice.

Telling Matteo that he could come in, she realized. He strode toward the bed, and his son. Alissandra smiled a little at how the baby gave him a solemn stare.

"Gian," said Matteo, and her smile deepened.

Chapter 12

Gian slept soundly in his cradle. Pale petals drifted from the orchard trees, over him and over his mother. Alissandra considered rising. For this early in spring, it was uncommonly warm, but she could see the first stars appearing in the deepening blue sky.

Someone moved, pale and ghostly, through the orchard. Her ladies-in-waiting—Lizina, perhaps—her mouth twisted. There was only so much time that a queen could spend alone. She stood.

And the figures were clear to her sight. Not her attendants, nor courtiers, nor servants. Bone white ladies—not those from the balls—indeed, with gazes far more feral and hungry on her.

Alissandra turned to snatch up Gian, but as her hands went out, a pair of pale hands interposed, and another pair hauled her back. The fingers gripping her were icy and strong as steel.

"O no, Your Majesty—you do not steal from us so easily."

The lady hauled her away from Gian, still sleeping as if enchanted, and into the center of their circle. Where Iolande stood, her face pale and strained, her plain clothing ragged.

"So they took you—that is why you vanished—"

Iolande smirked. It did not relieve the strain in her face, but it made Alissandra recoil.

"You always wanted to get your own way, Alissandra. They'll help me show you."

Alissandra's words froze in her mouth. She could not lift a finger, or so much as blink.

Iolande stripped off her own clothes, down to her shift. The ladies about Alissandra started to strip off hers, and piece by piece, leaving her only her shift, dressed Iolande as her. As Iolande tightened Alissandra's belt around her waist, suddenly she looked the image of Alissandra.

Alissandra found she could lower her arms. She stared at Iolande, and her triumphant face.

First she followed Esmeralda, thought Alissandra. Now she follows the ladies. She turned her face away. Iolande could always have followed Donata.

"A most regal and majestic queen," said a lady. "They will be glad to have so regal a consort."

Iolande smiled. Gian stirred and made a little grumpy noise. Iolande walked over and picked him up. Slowly, Gian roused, opening his solemn eyes to contemplate her.

Then he opened his little rosebud mouth to scream. And scream. And scream.

"Quick, away," said a lady. With icy cold fingers, they dragged her off, swiftly enough that Gian's wails died with distance, and she saw not another soul in the orchard. Mists folded round them.

"Hurry, make haste," said one lady, and the others took up, in sibilant whispers to make haste, make haste, and their steps grew faster, slipping her onward.

Mist thickened, hiding things only paces away. Even so, Alissandra could pick out twisted trees and lichen-covered rocks. No one could swiftly walk to such things from the doors of the castle—at least by unenchanted ways.

One more shape loomed from the mists: a house of gray stone, of flint. They hustled her within, and there, danced about her on the floor's flagstones, crowing with glee. The room was lit solely by a bowl of pale fire, which cast more shadows than light, but the racket of their rejoicing resounded from the stone walls—this was not the carriage, to be larger outside than in—and made her head ache. She shivered in the cold.

"The bowl!" cried one, and "The comb!" cried another, and a chorus ensued as all the ladies there called for them, at once, or in turn. The sound was too confused for her to hear them distinctly, most times, but one, with a flourish, produced a comb.

Ah, thought Alissandra, so they think to have their own way in all things. Slowly, she pulled the pins from her hair and shook her head, so that the locks tumbled down. The ladies eyed it avidly. She took the comb and, before their gazes, began to comb.

And comb. And comb.

Not so much as a bud fell down. Eyes narrowed. Mouths pursed. Their faces looked more like ferrets than human—

"I can only do it when I want." She lifted the comb. "And I can't want what I want to want."

Bone-white hand thrust a bowl of water before her. No towel, noted Alissandra, ironically. She held out the comb to her side, without glancing over. When it occurred to someone to take it, she plunged both hands into the water. Cold as the spring it had been drawn from. She washed. And washed. And finally drew her hands out, her fingers wrinkled like dried-out apples. She shook off what water she could and blew on them to warm them; they were white from cold, but the waters showed not so much as a white petal.

As if she would want lilies but not roses.

"No matter," said one lady. "We have shown her her place. That is what matters." But the words did not change the disgruntled expressions—not even of the lady who spoke.

* * *

Time passed.

They let her have a bed—worse than the one at the Princess's Rest—in an odd corner. They gave her drab clothes, enough to keep her warm, and they watched her every step from one corner or another.

She slept, she woke, she wandered about the ladies' flint house. Every now and again, one would try the comb on her again, or the bowl, but the light never changed, and she never saw any kind of clock. Her breasts ached.

From one window, she saw snakes writhing about in the mists. She wondered whether the ladies really kept them off. This flint house was not the ball, to draw the snakes by its glorious gleaming.

"They hate all things bright and beautiful," said a spiteful voice beside her. Alissandra turned. This pale lady was little more than a girl, short and slight, but her face held concentrated malice, and her hand held a comb.

"And you think I must think you wise enough to keep them off? What fools you are. You dragged me from my wailing child, and expect me to be happy enough to desire roses and lilies."

She bit down—in this dingy and gloomy house. They could brighten the house until it gleamed like the sun, the moon, and the stars, and still she would not want the flowers.

"I do not even know what his fate is!"

Light, careless laughter come from behind her. "Is that all?" Quick footsteps were followed by her hand being seized with icy fingers, by a lady no older than her questioner—who grabbed her other hand. They drew her along corridor after corridor, up and down stairs, until they came to where a pool spread on the floor. Its reflection was even darker than the house it showed, clouding her pallor, and that of the ladies.

"Salmon, o salmon," called out a lady imperiously.

The chorus arose, the ladies' words tripping over each other as they called to the salmon.

Alissandra could barely make out anything below the surface, but the shadowy shape of a fish did rise there. She bit her lip.

"Show us now what befell," said the lady.

Mists gathered over the pond. Slowly, slowly, as if scorning to answer—Alissandra's heart hammered so hard that she wondered if the ladies heard it, and she tried to keep her face smooth—but finally the pond was fogged over, without a trace of the scene before it.

Alissandra let her breath out. Ladies whispered with excitement, like girls gossiping at school, glancing from her to the pond and back. Alissandra turned her own gaze back to the pond.

The mists started to clear. The reflection was still dark, but she could make out the falling petals. She swallowed. The clearing mists seemed to slow. Moments inched by until she saw clearly a group of pale ladies bustling off a woman in her shift, and Iolande, in her clothes, with Gian in her arms, trying to soothe him. His arms only flailed more wildly, and Iolande scowled.

Lizina rushed through the orchard to her. Iolande looked up, managing to look despairing and distraught. Speaking—saying the baby just started to cry?

Lizina took him from her arms. He quieted, instantly. Iolande looked startled, and Alissandra wondered what the ladies had promised her.

The scene shivered. Mist returned—not thickly, but enough to blur. It showed more moments, with Gian wailing whenever Iolande came near. Iolande in her chamber, trying to sew, and doing it badly. Matteo—her heart ached doubly at how worn he looked, dreadful as the night when he had returned from the hunt.

"Enough," said one lady. The pond reflected them again. The lady turned, with the comb in her hand and a half-smile on her face.

"Enough folly," said Alissandra. "Are you not ladies? Is it not known to lands past thrice ten kingdoms than you are masters of seeming? Do you think me such a fool that I would trust what you showed me in such a pond? By bidding a *fish*?"

They recoiled, their breath hissing out, and stared at her with unblinking eyes.

* * *

Sibilant conversations in dark corridors, just past the range of her hearing, had ladies looking at her with sharp eyes. Once and only once did she come close enough to hear even a little: "Just because she can go out in daylight!" Finally, one conversation ended with a dozen grim-faced ladies stalking toward her.

"Come!" A lady held out a peremptory hand.

She came. There were enough of them to overpower her. Even, she realized as they hustled her out of the house of flint, more ladies than had first abducted her. And outside it was night again—

Her heart pattered. She told herself, again and again, that they would not just let her go free—the ladies had not let Matteo go free merely because she dragged him from the carriage—she had to keep her wits about her, and not be discouraged if a chance did not offer itself at once—but still her heart pattered.

All the more when they led her along familiar paths to a familiar door, up familiar stairs—she swallowed hard—without a familiar face about. As if the servants had been put to sleep by spell.

Then, the ladies would hardly have brought their prize here if they feared to lose her.

A mirror stood in the corridor, and for a moment, she glimpsed herself, more pale and ghostly than she had looked in the ladies' pool.

And then—into the nursery, where a nursemaid slept, and Gian slept. Sweeter than a rosebud, nestled in his crib. She crept closer, wondering if she should rouse him when he slept so soundly—and then he yawned, and kicked, and opened his solemn little eyes.

With a squeal of glee, he lifted chubby little arms. Moments later, she had him up and at her breast. Tears started to her eyes as she sat and let Gian nurse.

No one else in the castle stirred. She could only wonder where Matteo was—abed, asleep, no doubt. The ladies stood about her like steel pillars, all their gazes intent.

She held Gian in her lap, after. When something stirred outside the doors, he did not stare. Slowly, idly, she turned her head, and

met Lizina's gaze. After a moment, Lizina stole away, and Alissandra—idly—turned her attention back to Gian.

"Look!" said a lady, pointing outside. "The first light!"

Before they could tear him out of her arms with their icy fingers,
she laid Gian in his crib. The ladies had already formed a wall about her.
Slowly, with dignity, she walked with them. Down stairs, among trees,
down paths.

They had barely stepped over the threshold before a comb and
bowl were flourished before her. She lifted an eyebrow and took up the
comb.

They needed some hope to lure them on, she thought. Carefully,
she combed her hair. Once, twice, thrice—and the third time, a pure
red rose fell.

With squeals of glee, the ladies pounced. Their snatching fingers
had it torn to shreds within moments.

"Well?" said a lady, sulkily. "Go on."

She used every bit of skill she had to keep her face an impassive
mask as she combed, and combed, and combed. A hint of a smile
would ruin all. Solemn as a judge, she told herself, pulling a comb
through her hair, solemn, solemn—

It grew easier to maintain her countenance as their faces grew set in
rage and malice. "All night," one whispered, poisonously. "*All night.*"

She lowered the comb. "Once was not enough then, for more than
that."

The bowl was thrust under her nose. Mutely she washed, and a single lily, pure as starlight, floated on the waters. This time, they did not
destroy it, only watched it with avid eyes.

"We'll give you two more," said one lady, the words grated out.
"Then—you will learn what custom can do. We can wait until you learn
to be happy and content here. We can wait."

Alissandra lifted her head. "And you will get me stay until you see
the first signs of daylight," she said. "A moment or two will not suffice."

* * *

Her heart hammered.

Mists enfolded the orchards—now blossomless, but wild strawberry flowers, and white violets, and lilies of the valley bloomed pale along the path. Perhaps she should have told them that she needed to see Matteo, but she had to bargain so swiftly, without time for thought—

They swept her into the nursery, where Gian slept in his crib. In the back of the room, Matteo sat, so darkly clad he looked to be in mourning, haggard, and with a dreadful hope in his eyes. The ladies hissed and swirled about her. Some started to tug her back.

Slowly, with a great flourish, Matteo produced a feather—a feather as long as his forearm, iridescent even in this slight illumination. She swallowed. The ogre's feather from the Princess's Rest. Without so much as a glance at her, he made it shift through the air.

"O no, o no," spat one. "We're wise to that. You would steal what we have claimed—on the pretense that you had bought her—"

Nods and bitter agreement came all around.

"With those thrice-cursed mothers feigning that it is just," said one, poisonously.

Matteo spoke slowly and with care. "If you can not draw up a fair bargain, then we can not have one."

The feather shifted in his hand. The colors ran through it.

"Give us the feather. We will let you speak with her this night if you foreswear any more claim to her."

Alissandra bit her lip.

"I will give you this feather, and you will let me speak privately with her this night, and I will foreswear any further claim on her from this bargain."

Silence fell.

After a minute, a lady thrust out her hand. Solemnly Matteo handed over the feather. Alissandra hastened toward him—but Gian squirmed in the cradle, and she turned to pick him up before turning to Matteo. He drew her into a back corner.

"I knew—I knew," he whispered. "When Gian first wailed—I knew. Is there any hope?"

She drew her breath in and out and spoke as softly as she could. "They fear the daylight. Stop the clocks, exile the roosters, cover the windows with Donata's curtains. Do whatever you can to hide the approach of day until it is full come."

Matteo nodded, his face still grave. Not a lady twitched. But—she let her breath out—best not test their fortune with more chatter. Except—

"It will be my last visit, tomorrow."

He nodded again. She leaned against his shoulder.

One lady whispered, almost a hiss. "How sickeningly sweet."

* * *

Three roses, three lilies. She measured them out with care. And in the dark and the chill, they could not restrain themselves: they torn the blooms to pieces.

Alissandra could only wonder that they could crave the flowers of another lady's enchantment so.

* * *

They glided down the orchard path. They would hear her heart hammer. She could try to master her breath, steady her hands, keep her pace measured and her gaze on the path. She could do nothing for her heart.

But still they glided down, until they reached the door, and the still, silent corridors behind. Up the stairs. Into the nursery.

Matteo was there, in the back corner. The ladies drew themselves up, but he did not move forward, or indeed, at all. After her heart hammered a dozen times, Alissandra brushed by the ladies to take up Gian. And sit. With her back toward Matteo.

It took the ladies minutes to ease after that, but ease they did. Which was more than she could do. Gian fussed in her arms, but it would be hours, hours, before they could spring the trap. She could not even glance at the windows to see if she could tell whether it was starry sky or Donata's handiwork. If the ladies even guessed, they would haul her away, bargain or none.

She swallowed. Perhaps—perhaps Matteo had failed and came only to get a last glimpse of her before she was captive forever. Prudent and sagacious Matteo, keeping his face as stony as if he heard a case at court, hiding his thoughts from the ladies—and her.

Gian wailed and waved a tiny fist. Alissandra let out her breath and bent her attention to soothing him. Time had to pass. And pass. No clock chimed, no rooster crowed, no church bell rang. It gave her hope, but kept her ignorant of time passing as the ladies were.

Gian slept in her arms. She did not lay him down in the cradle.

One lady moved, restlessly. "It's been long. It's been too long."

"Till you see dawn light," said Alissandra, tranquilly.

Time passed, immeasurably.

"That was not a *bargain*," snapped another. "That was a fool of a queen talking as if it would win us over. Too foolishly indulgent, we have been. Haul her away, let her know we all granted her over-abundant generosity, far past her deserving and merits. She will learn to be happy to appease our indignation, and grant our desires."

Alissandra swallowed. Gian fussed, but she could pay him no heed. She looked up, past the ladies, into the corridor. There was light there—not candlelight or firelight but daylight—and where daylight could only shine after the sun was well-risen.

If she reckoned the window rightly.

She drew a deep breath and stood, holding Gian in one arm. The ladies smiled—smug, superior—and turned to go.

She took five steps to the window. Her free hand went out, and her fingers closed on cloth. Her heart leapt—they had, they had—and she tore back the curtain. Sunlight, clear and bright, flooded in from a cloudless sky, pouring slantwise over the room, catching every one of the ladies, and freezing their expression in inhuman, distorting rage. They did not twitch, not so much as a finger.

Gian seemed too startled to wail. She put her other arm about him.

Matteo leapt to his feet. He tore aside curtain after curtain, sending more floods of light toward the ladies. With the last curtain, the oldest lady cringed and folded in on herself. As at a signal, all of them shuddered and twisted—and began to shrink.

Lizina appeared in the doorway and, gravely, looked down. Alissandra swallowed and shifted Gian in her arms. The ladies were still shrinking, and changing color, and falling to the floor, until it was littered with toads and snakes and crawling creatures. Things glittered among them—she did not look closely enough to see what it was as she stepped back to keep Gian far away—and Lizina, with a nod, stepped aside, holding the door open, and herself as far away from it as she could without losing her grip.

A moment later, all the noisome creatures charged for the door. In spite of herself, Alissandra inched after. At the top of the stairs, she saw their desperate flight, writhing and wriggling, along the path and into the shade of the orchard.

"That will not suffice," murmured Lizina. "They will have to find graver darkness to not melt away in the sun."

Gian fussed, and she turned back to the room. Matteo, unsmiling, had gone down on one knee and take up the bright things that the ladies had let fall: four of them, all feathers. Silver, gold, fiery, and iridescent.

She swallowed, and went over to lay Gian in his crib. He fussed again, and she started to sing the lullaby. Matteo came over and laid down the feathers before slipping an arm about her waist and waiting.

The song ended, she leaned back against him for a precious moment, but—not all was done. And she still wondered.

"The same," she said. "The very same. How could those bone-pale ladies have the same feathers?"

"They could have been the same," said Lizina. "Perhaps their appearance at the balls was all glamour." She shrugged. "Perhaps they used you, Your Majesty, to center their spell. But as snakes and toads, they are no danger."

Alissandra sighed. "There's another who is," she said.

Matteo nodded gravely.

"It—she's my sister Iolande."

Matteo winced and looked at the feathers. "Her, first." His mouth twisted. "After, I shall send the feather back to the Princess's Rest."

"They may have all four, with my blessing," said Alissandra. "In gratitude."

Her thoughts returned to Iolande.

"She's still abed," said Matteo. "I shall have to make plans." He brooded a moment. "Stay here in the nursery. We shall swear the nursemaids to secrecy, for a few hours. And no doubt Lizina can keep watch."

* * *

Alissandra waited in the antechamber. With her hood up, her face was too shadowed to be seen by a passer-by, and her drab dress would not betray her. Still, she kept to the shadowed corner. She could only hear as her sister arrived in her own guise, as officials and courtiers and counselors greeted her. (Had Matteo and Lizina alone realized it was not her?)

Matteo let all the court settle before he spoke.

"I have a case before me that is uncommon in our laws. Tell me, if you think yourself wise, what should be done with a woman who consorted with ladies, so that they stole her sister away, and put the woman in her place?"

"She should be disinherited," said a grave old duke.

Other voices sounded, carefully primed: exiling her to the country, imprisoning her in a tower, burning her at stake, throwing her from a cliff—

A voice came—it was not Iolande's, and she could not recognize her own—"She should be touched with a toadstone and turned into a toad."

Alissandra winced.

"Even so," said Matteo coldly. "You have pronounced the sentence."

Silence reigned within.

Alissandra walked to the door. Lizina, standing there, helped off the cloak, and stood holding it. Alissandra walked into the throne room, where every courtier sat silent.

For a moment, it was as if a mirror sat beside Matteo. Then the glamour wavered, and faded. Between two breaths, the other woman was Iolande again, her face contorted with hatred.

She looked about, and she must have seen their faces. She jumped up, grabbed her skirt, and fled.

Courtiers gawked and stared, and with the back door so close to her, they were no obstacle to Iolande.

Matteo's voice thundered: "Guards!" Commotion roused, outside.

Minutes later—she had won her way to Matteo's side—a young guard, pale, appeared to drop to one knee and reported that the stranger in the queen's clothes had fallen from the stairs to her death, trying to escape.

Alissandra closed her eyes and clung to Matteo's arm.

"How *strange*," murmured an older noblewoman. "Many a maiden—even princesses—has won a prince after spending time as a frog."

Slowly, Alissandra opened her eyes. "Such frog princesses always know how to cook and sew, to impress their bridegrooms, and the fathers of their bridegrooms."

Epilogue

In sturdy independence, Gian walked into the room and up to the bed, where the baby lay beside Alissandra. Helena blinked her solemn eyes and looked back at her brother.

"Baby," said Gian firmly.

Matteo laughed. "Very good, Gian! I didn't know you knew the word."

Alissandra smiled on them all. Daylight made the room glow like a jewel. She glanced aside and saw Lizina watching them all. The sunlight shone through her pale hair, making it glow.

"Perhaps we should have a ball," said Alissandra, her voice low.

Matteo glanced over at her.

"You could have the pleasure of sitting out every dance. But when Lizina and I left my parents' castle, we pledged to share our fortune. And here I am with husband and children, and she has none—"

Lizina laughed. "You remember your promises well, Your Majesty. But it is not your only virtue." She smiled. Alissandra frowned a little; her face and pale gown seemed to glow as well as her hair, as if the sunlight shone through them as well. "Did you never learn the name of the woman whose burial you arranged for, paying her debts? It was Lizina."

Alissandra swallowed, hard.

"You shall not see me again for your lifetime, but you twain shall raise your son and your three daughters, and all of you be well."

And then there was nothing but light where she stood.

Gian eyed it curiously. So, it seemed, did Helena. And then, she could not tell when, it was all the brilliance of daylight.

Matteo slowly let his breath out. "So," he mused, "we have the name of the next princess ready, do we not?"

Alissandra nodded. "Lizina."

Appendix

For the curious, the source of the fairy tale allusions. Those fairy tales not identified by country are identified as closely as I got from my sources.

If you guessed what an allusion was, you may find this appendix disagrees. It does not necessarily you are wrong; many of the motifs and even plots are widespread.

All titles are those I found on variants I read.

Be warned that large portions of fairy tale plots are used, so this contains spoilers.

Chapter 1

locking up her sisters in the kitchen

The two older sisters in the Irish fairy tale "Fair, Brown, and Trembling" tried this on their youngest sister.

hunchbacked, with enormous eyes and swollen thumb

Three women like this appear in the Norwegian "The Three Aunts" and German "The Three Spinners."

spend every coin given to me for my dresses on some peasant lass's funeral

Spending money to allow a stranger to be buried appears in the Italian "Fair Brow" and the German "The Bird 'Grip'"

scrubbing pots in some kitchen

Princesses, and other heroines, looking for a job end up in the scullery, scrubbing away, in the English "Cap O'Rushes" and "Catskin", the Scottish "Rashen Coatie", the Norwegian "Kadie Woodengown", and the German "Maid Maleen" and "All Kinds of Fur."

hired by cats

A heroine seeks this job in the Italian "Colony of Cats."

seeking my fortune

A very common motif, as in the English "Three Heads in A Well" and "The Old Witch" and "Kate Crackernuts" and the Scottish "The Black Bull of Norroway."

hired to watch over a corpse

One girl who set out to seek her fortune got this job in the Scottish "The Girl and the Dead Man"

lay a trap for you here to tear you up with knives? Or broken glass

A man injured by these traps when trying to visit his beloved appears in the Italian "The Canary Prince" and "The Foppish King", the Russian "The Feather of Finist the Falcon", and the Danish "The Green Knight."

a ragged beggar girl

A character like this (and many of the events following from this in this chapter) feature in the French "Toads and Diamonds", the German "Frau Holle", and the Russian "Father Frost". It usually features two girls.

two girls who managed to pass their hidden tests, and one not

But not always. The German variant "St. Joseph in the Woods" features three girls, only one of whom does not manage.

anyone who tried to ape the first girl failed

The Mexican "Little Gold Star" also features three girls, but only one succeeded, and the other two failed.

I did not have to flee my father

Heroines run away from their fathers in the German "All Kinds of Fur", the English "Catskin", the Scottish "The King Who Wanted to Marry His Own Daughter," and the Italian "The Bear."

have the maidservant supplant me on the way

This happens to the heroine in the German "The Goose Girl."

an enchanted orange and then spent time trapped as a canary

All over Europe, from Spain to Russia, there are variants of "For the Love of Three Oranges" like this, though the fruit is not always the orange. The French "The Enchanted Canary" also features it.

a gown like all the flowers in the fields, another like all the birds in the air, and a third like all the stars in the sky

Demanding marvelous gowns is a common stalling tactic of princesses, and sometimes other heroines, as in the German "All Kinds of Fur" and the English "Catskin".

any talking calf

The Norwegian "Kadie Woodengown" was helped such a calf.

sent them off on impossible quest

Usually, it is the king who does this, but sometimes the princess does it in her own right, as in the French "King Fortunatus's Golden Wig" and the Russian "The Firebird and Princess Vasilisa."

ordered them to do impossible tasks

Again, this is usually the king, but sometimes the princess herself, as in the German "The Sea Hare."

asked impossible riddles and cut their heads off

This one can be either the king or princess, perhaps the princess more often, as in the Scottish "The Ridere of Riddles" and the German "The Riddle."

Chapter 2

save her seven brothers from a curse by keeping silent seven years

This task is needed in the Italian "Silent for Seven Years" and the German "The Seven Swans"

the chest that flew over land and sea

A demand made by the princess in "The King Who Wanted to Marry His Own Daughter."

engulfed in a black mist and whirled away

The fate of princesses in the Portuguese "What Came of Picking Flowers"

marry a man who rescued her

Among many, many, many others, this appears in the Norwegian "The Three Princesses of Whiteland", the Irish "The Thirteenth Son of the King of Erin", and the German "The Three Dogs."

Chapter 3

a princess who ran away from her father

Again, the German "All Kinds of Fur" and many others.

I said I could rescue the princesses

Such slander may force the hero to rescue her, as in the Norwegian "Dapplegrim."

spin a roomful of flax in a night

Similar slander featured in the Norwegian "The Three Aunts," for a different task.

seek your fortune

Again, the English "Three Heads in A Well" and many more.

offered half the kingdom to whoever it is that rescues Esmeralda and Iolande, and the whole after you die

Such an offer features in the Norwegian "The Seven Foals," the French "Three May Peaches," and the Scandinavian "Jesper Who Herded Hares."

the princess had a nose a foot long

The fate of one in the French "Damsel with the Long Nose"

To the first beggar who comes along

The fate of the princess in the German "King Thrushbeard."

I could have hidden in it, as a disguise

Such a disguise in used in the Italian "The Bear"

a marvelous beast and show me off at fairs

Something done in the Norwegian "Farmer Weathersky".

eating thistles raw

The heroine in the German "Maid Maleen" was reduced to this.

ogre

A common villain, such as in the French "Hop O' My Thumb" and the Italian "Thirteenth."

talking fox

This animal appears in the French "the Golden Blackbird", the Irish "The Greek Princess and the Gardener's Son," and the German "The Bird 'Grip'".

her husband the king found her in the forest without her hands

A incident occurring in the German "The Girl Without Hands", the Italian "Penta of the Chopped-Off Hands," and the Russian "The Armless Maiden."

it would to be a great princess

Such a promise was made in the Icelandic "Three Robes."

Queen Olivia had wished for any child, even a puppy,

It is always dangerous to make such a wish, as in the German "Hans My Hedgehog" and the Italian "The Apple Girl."

a milestone with the words carved in

The hero, and his brothers, all find one in the Russian "Tsaverich Ivan, The Gray Wolf, And The Firebird."

giant

A common villain, as in the English "Jack the Giant-Killer" and "Molly Whuppie."

dragon

A common villain, as in the German "The Two Brothers" and "The Three Dogs".

a wolf could carry both Prince Ivan and Helena the Beautiful

This wolf appears in the Russian "Tsaverich Ivan, the Gray Wolf, and the Firebird".

She put out her hand and caught it.

Aiding an animal often gains you some gain from them, as in the Hungarian "The Grateful Beasts."

the way to the bridegroom when the troll-wife is holding him captive

This is needed in the Norwegian "East of the Sun, West of the Moon", the Scottish "The Black Bull of Norroway," and many other tales.

no white clothes that would turn them back to swans

This appears in the widespread tales of the swan maiden, of course, but also in such fairy tales as the Russian "The Sea King and Vasilisa the Wise" and "Go To I Know Not Where, Bring Back I Know Not What."

Even for bandits

This features in the Norwegian "The Blue Belt."

Chapter 4

a talking horse to warn me

This horse appears in the French "King Fortunas's Golden Wig" and the Russian " The Firebird and the Horse of Power"

Scullery maid or the like

Again, as in "Catskin", "Cap O'Rushes", or "Kadie Woodengown."

sew and sell their wares

This is how, in the Russian "Vasilisa the Beautiful", the heroine lived for a time.

a traveler could stay the night by telling the tale of his journey

Such an inn features in the Danish "Niels and the Giants."

one brought her news of her husband

Another appears in the Greek "The Golden Crab," for just that reason.

what foreign princess brought that name to this country

It is the name of a princess in the English "Kate Crackernuts."

the oven had not asked her to do it

Such a request is made twice in the English "The Old Witch."

having been turned into a frog

The fate of a princess in "The Frog Princess," wide-spread over Europe.

Vasilisa the Wise

The heroine of the Russian "The Sea King And Vasilisa the Wise."

Vasilisa the Beautiful

The heroine of the Russian "Vasilisa the Beautiful"

Chapter 5

dance masters who had taught her to be light on her feet

As were taught the German and French "The Twelve Dancing Princesses"

she did the laundry whiter than clouds. Or snow. Or swans' wings

Incredible laundry skills appear in the Norwegian "East of Sun, West of Moon".

she married a crab—a golden crab

This, and the rest of the tale, is an animal bridegroom tale such as the Norwegian "East of the Sun, West of the Moon", coming closest to the Greek "The Golden Crab."

an ancestor who was freed by the burning of his animal skin

As befell in the Italian "The Pig King" and the German "Hans My Hedgehog."

a feather as long as Alissandra's arm

Ogres have been known to have feathers, as in the Italian "The Ogre's Feathers".

sisters or stepsisters

Two sisters adventure together in the Norwegian "Tatterhood"; stepsisters, in the English "Kate Crackernuts."

fools who steal enchanted treasures

As in the German "The Donkey, The Table, and the Stick."

his companion was an ugly soul, all hollow cheeked and pocked face, except for his marvelous glossy black hair

This character comes from the French "The Mangy Man". So does much of the tale after it.

the mangy man told the king

From "The Mangy Man" but also from the Norwegian "Dapplegrim" and the German "Ferdinand the Faithful and Ferdinand the Unfaithful."

a ship with three decks

Many a hero demands things to perform his tasks. This one appears in the Italian "The Ship with Three Decks."

Chapter 6

Princess Long-Nose

Again the French "The Damsel with the Long Nose."

a farmer's son who won a wizard's daughter's hand

This features in the American "King Marrack" and the Italian "The Billiard Players."

He's got a wishing hat! And a purse of gold—it's always full! And a horn that summons soldiers.

These objects, or some like them, feature in the Norwegian "Soria Moria Castle", the French "The Damsel With the Long Nose", and many others.

The thieves end up quarreling over who gets them,

Again, in "Soria Moria Castle."

he came to a mill that was not running

This, and many other events in the tale after, spring from the French "The Damsel with the Long Nose." Another like it is the German "Donkey Cabbages."

Even if the king did not need a loan

A way used in the Italian "Don Giovanni de la Fortune."

this daughter who would never tell the truth

This princess appears in the Norwegian "Boots Who Made The Princess Say, 'That's a story.'"

a daughter who never laughs

This princess appears in the German "The Golden Goose."

he's going hunting again

Venturing into the woods this way appears in the German "The Two Brothers" and the Indian "The King Who would be stronger than Fate."

Once there was a lad, his name was Jack

This, and much of the events that follow, follow a tale type that include the American "King Marrack", the Italian "The Billiard Players," the Russian "The Sea King and Vasilisa the Wise," the Norwegian "The

Maid Maleen", and many more. (But connecting the obstacles to the task is entirely my own invention.)

changing into a bird
An event in the German "Joringel and Jorinda"
escaping her evil father
Again, as in "Catskin", "Cap O'Rushes", or "All Kinds of Fur."
Chapter 7
In the middle of the courtyard stood a tree.
A moving tree appears in the German "One-Eye, Two-Eyes, and Three-Eyes."
Marya
A character in the Russian "Marya Morvena"
Talia
A character in the Italian "Sun, Moon, and Talia."
Kate
A character in the English "Kate Crackernuts"
Beauty With the Golden-Hair
A character in the French "Beauty With the Golden-Hair"
Rose-Red
A character in the German "Snow-White And Rose-red"
Catskins
A character in the American "Catskins"
Cap O'Rushes
A character in the English "Cap O'Rushes"
All Kinds of Fur
A character in the German "All Kinds of Fur"
Parsley
A character in the Italian "Parsley."
Anthousa Xanthousa Chrismalousa
A character in the Greek "Anthousa Xanthousa Chrismalousa"
turned into a bird
As in the German "Joringel and Jorinda."

a snow-white stag
A danger while hunting in the German "The Two Brothers."
Seven leagues boots
Used in the French "Hop O' My Thumb."
the youngest with a black bull
This happens in the Scottish "The Black Bull of Norroway."
Our king and queen had three sons
This begins a wide-spread tale type, such as the German "The Singing Bone" and the Greek "The Singing Bagpipes."
to a ball as a challenge to a master thief
Tales of challenges between a king or someone else of high rank and a master thief are widespread, though not all involving stealing things at a ball.
arriving late is proper. Midnight, say
In the English fairy tale "Tattercoats", the heroine arrives at midnight.
the family, the ones we heard of, that the robbers got
This family comes from the German "The Old Woman in the Woods" as does much of the tale she tells.
the bride to declare she'd gone to the woods after him
This happens in the German "The Robber Bridegroom" and the English "Mr. Fox."
Eulalie
A character of this name appears in the French "Jean, the Soldier, and Eulalie the Devil's Daughter."
a queen was married and had a son
This begins like the Hungarian "The Gold-bearded Man."
a great golden bird
This bird appears in the French "Georgic and Merlin."
They hired him to help the gardener
This or like tasks appear in "The Gold-bearded Man" and the German "Iron Hans."

the overripe peach to the oldest princess, the just ripe one to the middle princess, and the green one to the youngest princess

The fruit, and the precise meaning of the riddle (according to the princesses' ages), vary but appear in both the Romanian "The Foundling Prince" and the Greek "The Magician's Horse."

how a soldier had been lost in the woods and come to an ogre's house

This, and the events after, feature in the French "Jean the Soldier and Eulalie the Devil's Daughter," and the Norwegian "Master Maid."

Chapter 8

a wedge of swans, carrying a carpet

This occurs in the German "The Seven Swans."

a doe that turned into a woman

This occurs in the French "The Hind in the Wood."

the hind is leading him to a grave

This appears in the British "The Famous Flower of Serving Men."

the heir's been promised to the wildman

A promise made in the Slavonic "King Kojata," the Scottish "The Battle of Birds," and the Estonian "The Grateful Prince."

Carla brought a bundle. Cloth by its weight

This features in the English "Catskin", the German "All Kinds of Fur", and the Scottish "The King Who Wanted to Marry His Own Daughter."

he had found a castle and woken an enchanted lady, and visited her and his children

This arrangement appears in the Italian "Sun, Pearl, and Anna."

She had not brought ball gowns, but perhaps she was not the only princess drudging away in a hot kitchen in the kingdom.

This features in the English "Catskin", the German "All Kinds of Fur", and the Scottish "The King Who Wanted to Marry His Own Daughter."

those wild men never let any beast escape alive

This features in the German "Iron Hans."

Or a witch instead
This appears in the Russian "The Witch" or the German "The Old Woman In The Woods."

A golden stag
This allures a huntsman in the German "The Two Brothers."

that rat-catcher
This character appears in the German "The Pied Piper."

a hero had to rescue some princess by enduring the torments of goblins until midnight
This appears in the French "The Little Soldier," the German "The Raven," and "The Blue Mountains"—source unidentified in the work where I read it.

King Matteo's grandmother had come to the ball at midnight, in rags
This appears in the English "Tattercoats."

I will stay up to see to it
This task occurs in the English "Kate Crackernuts."

a talking fox
This animal appears in the French "the Golden Blackbird", the Irish "The Greek Princess and the Gardener's Son," and the German "The Bird 'Grip'".

Chapter 9
king's unending illness
The problem of a prince the English "Kate Crackernuts."

golden apples
These appear in the Russian "The Bold Knight, the Apples of Youth, and the Water of Life."

the water of life
This appears in the German "The Water of Life."

a golden blackbird
This appears in the French "The Golden Blackbird."

masters of the healing arts

These appear in the Italian "The Canary Prince," and the French "Damsel with the Long Nose" and "The Two Brothers".

the golden stag in the forest

This allures a huntsman in the German "The Two Brothers."

dragons

One features in both the German "The Two Brothers" and "The Three Dogs."

witches

This appears in the Russian "The Witch" or the German "The Old Woman In The Woods."

unicorns

One appears in the German "The Little Tailor."

a nephew could be his heir

A solution in the French "The Bee and the Orange Tree."

Chapter 10

Neither for silver nor for gold, neither for wish nor for charm.

Refusing to sell except for her own wish features in the Russian "The White Wolf," the Norwegian "East of the Sun, West of the Moon," and the German "The Singing, Springing Lark."

see all their finery as they arrive

A subject discussed in the English "Tattercoats."

The first dance was frantic of step

This is not so much a fairy tale as part of British folklore of what seeing them dancing was like—hectic.

Not to eat or drink

Fairy food was dangerous to eat in British folklore.

Then they shoved him into the arms of another partner.

This, and many of the other incidents after, feature in the English "Kate Crackernuts."

After my mother died, my father said that we three girls had to keep house

Many of the events here feature in the American "Little Catskin."

princesses who speak rudely to great ladies
An incident in the French "Diamonds and Toads."
held him through any enchantment could they seize him
An incident in the British "Tam Lin."
These three sold me for feathers. This one bought me. To whom do I belong?
A similar question is posed in the Russian "The White Wolf."
Chapter 11
not some servant who turned the princess into a bird and claimed her place
As in "For the Love of Three Oranges", found all over Europe.
their rights to have all of a dead woman's debts paid before they buried her
A demand made in the Italian "Fair Brow" and the German "The Bird Grip."
seek our fortunes
As in the Norwegian "The Seven Foals."
It only put out one rose at a time
As in the Italian "Rag and Bones". Other means of marrying off princesses to the first passerby have also appeared.
when a great wind blew him far, far, far off course
As in the Russian "Good Advice."
Chapter 12
handsome young man, dressed as finely as they were
This, and much of the rest of his story, are like the English "Tatter-coats."
Aunt Donata—at least, she approved of my sewing
This, and much of the rest of his story, come from the Norwegian "The Three Spinners."
His name was True
This, and much of the rest of the story, comes from the Norwegian "True and Untrue."

Chapter 13

like a swan maiden

A figure in the Swedish "The Swan Maiden" and the German "The Three Swan."

Your great-great-grandfather was uncommonly prudent

As in the American "King Marrack" and the Russian "The Sea King and Vasilisa the Wise."

the hag said, "It can't be."

Such a trick works in the Italian "King of Love" and the British "Willie's Lady," though the purpose is not quite the same.

half the kingdom now and all after he dies

As in the Norwegian "The Seven Foals" and the Irish "The Greek Princess and the Young Gardener."

Chapter 14

a king tries to add conditions

As the king tries in the Norwegian "Dapplegrim."

he kissed a donkey

The fate of the king in the Scandinavian "Jesper Who Herded Hares."

magically bound to ferry travelers

The fate in the German "The Griffin."

He could end up dead

The fate in the Hungarian "The Grateful Beasts".

on a glass mountain

Done in the Norwegian "The Glass Mountain."

the first passer-by

Done in the German "King Thrushbeard."

just have the young men line up and have you and Iolande each hand one a golden apple

Done in the French "Little Johnny Sheepskin."

A captive of horrible monsters

A fate in the Norwegian "The Three Princesses of Whiteland" and the Portuguese "What Came of Picking Flowers." Among others.

to get some wool

A technique used in the Greek "Psyche and Cupid."

set out to seek their fortunes

A very common motif, as in the English "Three Heads in A Well" and "The Old Witch" and "Kate Crackernuts" and the Scottish "The Black Bull of Norroway."

three enchanted oranges

As in the widespread tale "For the Love of Three Oranges."

Queen Maleen

The events mostly follow the French "Maid Maleen."

Trolls

As in the Norwegian "Three Princesses of Whiteland"

dragons

As in the Bukovanian "The Flower Queen's Daughter"

a dragon

As in the German "The Two Brothers" or "The Three Dogs."

the ferryman must bear passengers

As in the German "The Gryphon"

how his fool daughter would lavish it on a peasant's son

As in the Russian "Lucky Vasily"

His great-granddaughter Catherine

As in the Italian "Catherine and Her Fate".

Chapter 15

turned to stone

This occurs in the German "The Queen Bee" and the Norwegian "The Giant Who Had No Heart In His Body."

he found the ring inside it

This occurs in the English "The Fish and The Ring."

filled it with salt for cargo

This occurs in the Russian "The Salt Mountain."

dressed in a gown like all the clouds in the sky
Such gowns appear in the German "All Kinds of Fur" and the English "Catskin".
wishes for the child
They can be dangerous, as in the German "The Juniper Tree" and "Hans My Hedgehog," and the Italian "The Myrtle."
always do what the child asks of you
From the Danish "The Green Knight"
to a woman as lovely as I am
From the German "All Kinds of Fur."
or one who could wear something of mine
From the Scottish "The King Who Wanted to Marry His Own Daughter."
or to make sure the stepmother does not take charge of my child by locking up him up in a tower
From the Irish "The Black Knight and the Thief of the Glen"
never marry again except to a great princess
From the Icelandic "The Three Robes."
miller's daughters
The heroine of the German "The Girl Without Hands"
gardener's boys
The heroes of the Irish "The Greek Princess and the Young Gardener", the French "The Twelve Dancing Princesses," and the German "Iron Hans."
the wolves did not eat her
This happens in the German "Brother and Sister."
she does not end up married to a cobbler
This happens in the English "The Three Heads in the Well."
Chapter 16
hauled her away from Gian
A scene much like this features in the Icelandic "The Witch in the Stone Boat."

And scream. And scream
A reaction as in the Finnish "The Wonderful Birch."
a house of gray stone, of flint
A house like this appears in the English "Sir Gaffer Vams."
Salmon
One appears in the Scottish "Gold-tree and Silver-tree."
past thrice ten kingdoms
A common turn of phrase in Russian fairy tales, such as the Russian "The Frog Princess".
into the nursery, where a nursemaid slept, and Gian slept
As in the German "Brother And Sister."
Stop the clocks, exile the roosters, cover the windows with Donata's curtains
The directions also appear in the Italian "The Prince in the Henhouse."
what should be done
A request made in the German "The Goose Girl."
turned into a toad
A fate in the widespread tale "The Frog Princess."
Epilogue
The secret is also revealed in the German "The Bird 'Grip.'"

Also by Mary Catelli

Free Passage
Isabelle and the Siren
Journeys And Wizardry
Lifestone
Magic of the Lost God
Never Comment On A Likeness
One Name
The Drunken Mermaids
The Turtle in the Sea of Sand
Were I You
Where There Is Smoke
Through A Mirror, Darkly
The Princess Seeks Her Fortune